Web of Deceit

Web of Deceit

Peter Conway

ROBERT HALE · LONDON

ISBN 978-0-7090-9102-8

Robert Hale Limited
Clerkenwell House
Clerkenwell Green
London EC1R 0HT

www.halebooks.com

Typeset in 11½/16pt New Century Schoolbook
by Derek Doyle & Associates, Shaw Heath
Printed in Great Britain by the MPG Books Group,
Bodmin and King's Lynn

CHAPTER ONE

Richard Kershaw lifted up the beautifully crafted, one in twelve scale, circular, miniature dining table top and held it against the powerful adjustable light on his work bench. Through the magnifying lenses of his glasses, he inspected it from every angle and then checked the diameter all the way round with his callipers, nodding his head slightly with satisfaction at the result as he screwed it on to its three-legged base. It was a beautiful piece, he thought, even if he had to be the one to say so. He had carved it lovingly in mahogany and it was a perfect size for the dining room in the Victorian dolls' house, which he had painstakingly restored for his granddaughter over the preceeding two years.

Working with his hands, be it in the operating theatre or during his leisure time, was one of the two greatest pleasures of his life and this piece of woodwork was as good as if not better than anything he had ever done before. All it needed now was to be polished and then he would be able to start on the four chairs, which would perhaps be an even greater challenge. He glanced at his watch, saw that it was just 4.15 and got to his feet. Parker was as obsessional as he was himself and tea would be brought into the drawing room just as the hall clock was striking the half hour and it would never do not to be waiting in the upright chair by the window.

Leaving the piece on his worktable, he got to his feet and started to descend backwards down the almost vertical wooden steps to the garage. He had just put his leading foot onto the concrete floor, when he heard a sound behind himself and had just started to turn his head when there was a blinding flash of light in front of his eyes and he fell backwards.

Chief Superintendent Tyrrell was writing a report in his office at Scotland Yard when the buzzer sounded on his desk.

'Commander Maxton to see you, sir,' his secretary said.

Tyrrell let out a muffled curse under his breath. 'Thank you, Mary. Show him in, would you, please?'

He got to his feet as the burly, middle-aged man came in and made a gesture towards the chair in front of the desk. 'Cup of coffee, sir?'

The man shook his head as he sat down. ' 'Fraid I can't spare the time. I'm due to see the Commissioner at 10.30 and that's what I wanted to have a word with you about. No doubt you've already seen or heard that one of the top neurosurgeons at St Gregory's Hospital, one Richard Kershaw, was murdered last weekend and, knowing the good reputation that your team has for dealing with the medical profession, I'd like you to come along with me. My secretary has downloaded some stuff on the man from the Internet and also made a copy of his entry in *Who's Who* and perhaps you'd care to look at them before the meeting?'

The man took a folder out of his briefcase and handed it across the desk.

'Thank you, sir. I'll take a look at it right away and see you in the Commissioner's office.'

Tyrrell was pretty sure that Maxton was little more than a messenger. Presumably, he thought, the man must have been at one time more than the pompous penpusher that he was now, but there was little sign of it. At least, though, Tyrrell thought, if he played his cards correctly, this might be an opportunity, the first for many months, for him to get some work on the ground.

The Commissioner's instructions were characteristically brief and to the point. 'As you will have seen from the bumpf that Maxton gave you,' he said, 'the forensic people are quite convinced that this fellow Kershaw's death could not possibly have been due to an accident. The nature of his head injury makes it quite clear that he was hit on the back of his head by some form of blunt instrument. Now, he was a top man in his field and there is the added complication that he was married to a member of the aristocracy, the sister of an earl. His widow, one Lady Elizabeth Kershaw, is at present looking after her grandchildren out of London, while her son and daughter-in-law are on holiday in Europe and refuses to have anything to do with the media. Inevitably that is going to present them with a challenge and make them sharpen their pencils, but I

7

can't see her changing her mind and, as Seymour is clearly out of his depth, the situation clearly calls for a senior officer like you with experience of working with the medical profession to take over. The scene-of-crime people have finished in the London property where the murder took place and Lady Kershaw's manservant is looking after the house, so you will have a clear field there. Keep me in close touch with how you get on, and if you require any extra help let me know.'

'Of course, sir.'

Tyrrell knew that his two assistants, Inspectors Mark Sinclair and Sarah Prescott would have the essentials at their fingertips very soon after he had told them briefly about the case and instructed them to have a word with Jack Pocock, the head of the scene-of-crime team, which had been at the site, and to report back to him an hour later.

When the two detectives returned, Sarah said: 'Jack will be available to show the site to all of us at your convenience, sir. Evidently the murdered man, one Richard Kershaw, a well-known neurosurgeon at St Gregory's Hospital, lived with his wife in a detached house in Highgate. When he bought it soon after he married about thirty years ago, he added a detached garage with a workshop above it. Woodwork, particularly the making of dolls' house furniture, was his main hobby and he was working on a piece up there last Sunday afternoon. He's well known for being a stickler for punctuality and when his manservant went to investigate when his employer was late for tea, he found him lying at the base of the steep, wooden staircase leading to the loft, with an obviously serious head injury. Feeling faint himself at the sight and knowing at once that he wouldn't be able to do anything about it directly, he hurried back to the house, telephoned for an ambulance and it was the crew, finding the man dead, who sent for us.'

'Was anyone else in the house at the time apart from the manservant?'

'Evidently not, sir. There are no other resident staff and Kershaw's wife, Lady Elizabeth, has been looking after her two grandchildren in her son's house in Hertfordshire while their parents were trekking in the Tartra mountains in Poland and she has been unable to contact them. They are due back at the end of the week.'

'Know anything about the manservant?'

'Nothing apart from the fact that he's in his early sixties and has been with the Kershaws all their married life.'

'Thank you, Sarah. Anything to add, Mark?'

'Not a great deal, sir, I'm afraid. Tredgold did the autopsy, but he was out on a case when I rang, and that long-suffering secretary of his, Miss Graves, was, as usual, very cagey and wouldn't even confirm the cause of death over the phone, saying that her boss would give us the details when we saw him. We have an appointment with him first thing tomorrow.'

'St Gregory's rings a bell with me. Didn't the daughter of that psychiatrist, who was murdered by his adopted son, work there,' Tyrrell said.

'Yes, sir, you're quite right. Rebecca Cochrane's her name. As I'm sure you remember, she was very helpful to us and if she's still at St Gregory's she might well be able to give us some background information, on an informal basis, as to what this man Kershaw was like.'

'Yes, but with your experience, I'm sure I don't need to tell you that one has to tread very carefully at hospitals.'

'Exactly, sir, and for that reason I had in mind that Sarah and I should tackle the senior administrator and the chairperson of the medical staff committee first.'

'Good idea and I'm quite happy for you both to do that, but first, I suggest that we get Jack Pocock to show us where the murder took place and then take it from there.'

Jack Pocock's car was parked in the drive of the house in Highgate, and as they pulled up behind it the scene-of-crime man came down the steps from the front door.

'Anyone at home, Jack?' Tyrrell said.

'Only the manservant and the gardener, who is at present working on the flowerbeds in the back garden, sir. As I explained to Inspector Sinclair, the former likes to be called just by his surname, Parker. He looks just like one of those gents' gents I've seen in revivals of those old pre-war films and I doubt if we'll get much out of him. I'll introduce him after I've shown you the garage where the murder took place.'

The garage was built of brick and completely separated from the house by a path leading to the back garden, which was blocked by a gate set into a wooden frame a good nine feet high. It was a substantial building, wide enough to accommodate two cars, and there was an area behind the parking spaces, which contained a wooden staircase leading up to the loft.

Between that and the back wall were a motor-driven lawn mower and other gardening equipment.

Pocock took a photograph out of his briefcase and handed it to Tyrrell.

'As you see, sir, the body was lying on its back with the feet close to the staircase and the back of the head resting on the concrete floor. The staircase is very steep and it looks as if the victim was coming down backwards and had just reached the floor when he received a massive blow on the top of his skull. It seems almost certain that the murder weapon was the length of tubular scaffolding shown in this picture, and here is another view of it resting against the inside of the back wall of the garage as we found it. It has been removed for detailed examination. The DNA of the blood and the other tissue on it, and also any fingerprints, aren't available yet.'

Tyrrell looked at the picture carefully and then handed it over to his two assistants.

'Presumably, Jack, the garage was open when this fellow Parker found the body.'

'Yes, sir. The side door, which is normally kept locked, was open and the up and over electrically operated one at the front was locked shut. I'll leave Parker to tell you the details as far as he is concerned. The key to the side door was found in the dead man's trouser pocket.'

'Who else has a key?'

'Just his wife, Lady Elizabeth, and the gardener who comes twice a week. There is space for two cars and that afternoon Kershaw's BMW was there, but Lady Elizabeth had taken her vehicle to her son's place where, I believe, she is looking after her two grandchildren.'

11

'Have you seen the gardener yet, Jack?'

'Yes, sir, and perhaps you'd like to have a word with him yourself before going into the house.' The scene-of-crime man pointed up the staircase. 'While you are here, sir, may I suggest that you take a look at the workshop above?'

The room at the top of the stairs was spacious and, in addition to the strip lighting in the roof, there was an anglepoise light on the workbench on which were also a number of tools and a miniature, circular mahogany dining table, which Kershaw had clearly been about to start polishing with the equipment there.

'What an amazing piece of work,' Tyrrell said. 'I remember going to an exhibition of dolls' house furniture at a National Trust house a few years back and this is as good as anything I saw there. Just look at the detail on the legs.'

The dolls' house for which the table was obviously destined was sitting on the table set at right angles to the workbench and was also made of wood. It was a substantial structure roughly seventy-five centimetres high and a hundred and fifteen wide and it had three front panels, which were hinged and were secured by small metal hooks, which could be set into eyes screwed into the main fabric of the building. The panels were standing open and it was possible to see into the sitting room, the dining room and kitchen on the ground floor with a staircase leading up from the hall. On the floor above were three bedrooms and the bathroom. All the rooms had windows with metal frames, which could all be swung open. There were some china fittings such as the sink in the kitchen and the bath and lavatory upstairs, but all the furniture, with the exception of the upholstered sofa and armchairs were made out of beautifully carved wood.

'Apart from the furniture, the carpets and rugs are also works of art in their own right and I wonder if Lady Elizabeth was responsible for stitching them,' Sarah said.

'I wouldn't be surprised and I'm sure this fellow Parker will be able to tell us.' Tyrrell said. 'Why don't we go down now and have a word with him after we've seen the gardener? I know you've talked to both of them already, Jack, but I'd like to hear their stories in their own words and also get my impression of the two of them. Perhaps you'd ask the gardener to come here first and then we'll see Parker in the house and I'll get you to show us round afterwards. I'd rather you didn't let the man know that we were here beforehand, as I'd like to see his reactions to our arrival.'

Fred Stacey was a heavily-built, middle-aged man with a ruddy complexion, who removed his battered cap as Pocock ushered him into the area of the garage where Kershaw's body had been found.

'Sorry to have interrupted your work, Mr Stacey,' Tyrrell said when he had introduced himself and his two colleagues, 'but I'm sure you understand that we need to talk to everyone helping to run the house and grounds.'

'That's all right, sir. Me back's givin' a bit of trouble and I could do with a break.'

'How long have you been working here?'

'Must be all of twenty year, sir. Nice people 'ere. Lady Elizabeth allus takes an interest in the garden and

13

knows a lot about plants. As for Mr Kershaw, I never saw much of 'im as 'e were allus at the 'ospital when I came, but 'e allus made a point of seeing me whenever our paths crossed and gave me a generous present at Christmas.'

'What did you do for Mr Kershaw personally?'

'Just gave 'is car a good clean each Wednesday when 'e took Lady Elizabeth to the 'ospital and checked the oil and tyres regular like. The garage people used to collect it whenever it needed a service. Very particular about 'is car was Mr Kershaw.'

'So you didn't see him all that often?'

'No, sir, but 'e were allus pleasant when I did.'

'How about Mr Parker?'

' 'E's a caution is Mr Parker. I thought 'e were proper stuck up when I first meet 'im, but 'e ain't like that at all and we always meet for a cup of tea in the kitchen midmorning and 'ave a chat.'

'I'm sure you know that Mr Kershaw was killed by a blow on the head from the piece of scaffolding that we found propped up against the wall over there. Do you know where it came from?'

'Fahnd it meself, didn't I? It were in the undergrowth near them trees behind the garage an' I put it inside against the wall, meanin' to get rid of it, but I didn't get rahnd to it.'

'When was that?'

'Must 'ave bin abaht a month ago or so.'

The front door to the house was closed and in response to Tyrrell's ring on the bell, it was opened by a slightly built man of medium height, with neatly cut grey hair, who looked to be in his early sixties. He was wearing a white shirt and a black tie to go with a suit of the same colour, the trousers of which looked as if they had been pressed that morning and his black shoes had been polished to a mirror-like finish.

'Good morning,' Tyrrell said. 'You must be Parker. I believe you've already met Mr Pocock. My name is Roger Tyrrell and my two assistants are Inspectors Sarah Prescott and Mark Sinclair.'

'I'm very pleased to see you, sirs, and you, madam. May I show you into the drawing room?'

'You certainly may and perhaps you'd be good enough to stay as we would like to have a word with you.'

Sinclair couldn't help admiring his senior's approach to the man, who obviously approved of both Tyrrell's immaculate appearance and cultured voice, as he led them in through the door on the right side of the hall.

'I gather that you are the only member of the family here at present, Parker,' Tyrrell said, looking directly at the man who was standing between them and the door, stooping slightly and with his legs together.

'Yes, that is the case, sir. Lady Elizabeth is looking after her two grandchildren while her son and daughter-in-law are on holiday abroad. They are camping somewhere in Eastern Europe and she has not been able to contact them since the tragedy occurred. I spent a few days with her in Hertfordshire and then she asked me if I would return here to keep an eye on the place while your team were inspecting the grounds. I took the liberty of telephoning her this morning as soon as I heard that you would be coming today and I will, of course, give you her number as she indicated that she would be willing to speak to you should that be necessary. I hope I did right, sir?'

'You have no need to worry on that score, Parker,' Tyrrell said. 'You have coped admirably.'

'Thank you, sir. I am very relieved to hear you say that. I always try to do what is best for Lady Elizabeth. I have known her since she was a child and have the very greatest respect for her.'

Tyrrell nodded and smiled. 'Mr Pocock had already told us something about your part in this sad event, but it would help us greatly to hear it again in your own words and we may have some questions to ask you as well. Why not sit down over there?'

The man cleared his throat and perched awkwardly on the very edge of the chair, looking straight at the detective.

'Mr Kershaw,' he said, 'was a gentleman to whom punctuality was extremely important. Whenever he was here on his own at weekends, if he asked for tea to be brought at four-thirty, then that was when he liked it, not a minute early, not a minute late. At precisely that time last Sunday I knocked on the door and when there was no answer, I tried again and then opened it. There was no one in here and, after putting the tray down on that table there, I went back to the kitchen and waited for a further five minutes, leaving the door open so that I might hear him coming in. When there was still no sign of him I went out into the garage to see if he was all right and that's when I found him lying on his side at the base of the staircase in there.

'I worked as a farm boy before I took up service with the Marquis and I saw enough animals in that state to know that he was dead. I decided not to touch him, went back to the house as fast as I could and rang for an ambulance. I thought that he must have slipped on coming down the steps and landed on the concrete on the back of his head, but I knew that I must have been wrong directly the attendants called for the police.'

'Did Mr Kershaw normally wash and change before taking his tea?'

'It depended on whether he was intending to continue his work afterwards or not, sir. If Lady Elizabeth was here, he would usually take a shower and change before having tea with her, but if he was on his own, he often continued working afterwards and under these circumstances, he would merely take off his overall and wash his hands in the downstairs cloakroom, leaving his shower until later.'

'Would you normally hear him come in?'

'No, sir. The kitchen is right at the back of the house and I am also a little hard of hearing these days.'

'Am I right in assuming that the only residents here were Mr Kershaw, Lady Elizabeth and yourself?'

'That is the case, sir.'

'What about non-resident staff?'

'There is a cleaning lady who comes here every morning at 9 a.m., except at weekends. Lady Elizabeth's secretary attends twice weekly to deal with her correspondence and e-mails and the gardener also comes twice a week on Tuesdays and Thursdays.'

'And your duties?'

'I look after Mr Kershaw's wardrobe and am responsible for cooking the breakfast, which is served at seven-thirty each morning and also the evening meal except when there are guests when a young woman, who runs a catering firm, provides it, although I always serve it myself. I also deal with telephone calls and the tradesmen, as well as making sure that domestic supplies are kept up to date. I also have control of the household budget.'

'What happened if Mr Kershaw was operating late?'

'That was quite a frequent occurrence, sir. He often used to spend those nights in his flat near the hospital, which he also used as an office for his private secretary. He always telephoned in good time, though, to let Lady Elizabeth know if that was going to be the case.'

'Thank you, Parker,' Tyrrell said, 'that was all very clear.' There was a long pause. 'I understand from Mr Pocock that you have worked in many capacities for a very long time for Lady Elizabeth and her family and I have no doubt that you are the soul of discretion and feel great loyalty to them. However, Mr Kershaw has been murdered and it is also your duty as a citizen to tell us anything that may help us to find the person responsible. That will mean giving us information about the Kershaw family, and that includes Lady Elizabeth.'

There was another even longer pause. 'I quite understand, sir, that that is the case, but I wonder if I might telephone Lady Elizabeth as I feel unable to discuss the family behind her back.'

Tyrrell smiled. 'Of course, you must do that and when you have finished I'd like to have a word with her myself. You see, I would be more than willing to drive out to Hertfordshire to see her at her convenience and I would like to make that arrangement with her as soon as possible.'

The man nodded. 'Thank you, sir. I'll telephone her straight away and I'll ask her to hold on when I've finished.'

Sinclair looked across at Sarah Prescott and, after Parker had left the room, raising his eyebrows fractionally, while Tyrrell got out of his chair to inspect the photograph on the grand piano. It was of a rather austere-looking man standing stiffly to attention in court dress, with a ceremonial sword at his left side. A good five minutes went by before the manservant came back and made a gesture towards the detective with his hand, who followed him into the hall.

'There are no problems, I'm glad to say, and Lady Elizabeth is happy to see me tomorrow morning,' Tyrrell said, when he returned with the manservant. 'She is staying at her son's house near Hatfield and is quite happy for Parker to give us some background information about himself, but she would prefer to discuss any family matters with me face to face, which I fully understand.' He made a gesture towards the upright chair near the piano. 'Perhaps, Parker, you would like to sit down over there?'

After the manservant had reached the chair, he sat on the very edge of it, looking profoundly uncomfortable as Tyrrell addressed him again.

'Now,' he continued, 'perhaps, as a start, you might give us some idea of the sort of person Mr Kershaw was?'

After a moment or two, the man looked rather more at ease and began.

'Mr Kershaw was a very clever and gifted man with

great charm. I was working for Lady Elizabeth's father when he died and that was when her mother went to live with her elder son and, as he had his own staff, it was clear that I would have no place in that household. I had always got on well with Lady Elizabeth and when she asked me if I would consider working for her, I was only too happy to agree and I'm sure that her mother had a hand in that suggestion herself. You see, the Marchioness used to tell me a lot of things, knowing that I would never betray her confidences, and I think she saw me as a way of keeping in contact with her daughter and later on her twin grandchildren.'

'How did you get on with Mr Kershaw yourself?'

'To start with he seemed to think that my presence in this house was both curious and amusing, but one Sunday, when I was alone with him and had brought him his tea, he asked me to sit down and tell him about myself. When he discovered that both my parents had been killed in a road accident in the 1950s, that I had no other relatives and that I had been at a Barnado's home, he became really interested. I explained that when I was fifteen, I got a job as gardener's assistant at the Marquis's estate in Surrey. Lady Elizabeth was seven or eight years old at the time and I often used to see her in the garden. She had a little plot of her own and, in addition to helping her with that, I used to push her on the swing, which was attached to a branch of one of the trees, until she got the hang of it herself. I also taught her the names of the flowers, shrubs and trees. Rather than sending her to school, her parents employed a resident governess and, as a result, she missed out on normal friendships with other children and the normal games and pleasures that most children enjoy, and I like to think that I was able to remedy some of those deficiencies.

'Although I got on well with Henry Russell, the head gardener, and tried my best, both of us knew by the time I was seventeen that I was too small and slightly built to be suited for working on the land. He had a word with the butler and that's when my work was transferred to the house. I was taken on as a junior footman and gradually rose to become the Earl's valet, which was the position I held when he died, which he did very soon after Lady Elizabeth and Mr Kershaw were married.

'At that time, Lady Elizabeth asked me what I planned to do as she knew that the new Earl wanted staff of his own and I explained that I would be out of a job. That was how I came to be offered the position of manservant here.'

'After you moved here, how did you get on with Mr Kershaw?'

'It would be presumptuous of me to comment on that, sir, but he always seemed to appreciate the little services I was able to offer him.'

'Which were?'

'I kept his clothes clean and in order and on the mornings he went to work, I laid out the suit he was to wear, provided a clean shirt and underwear, a suitable tie and made sure that his shoes were highly polished. At first, he used to make little jokes about what his colleagues would say if they knew that he had a personal valet, but then he started to make appreciative comments about the way I cared for him.

Initially, too, he often made fun about people with titles and the aristocracy in general, but fairly recently, from the questions he asked me, I began to wonder if he had ambitions to be knighted himself, particularly after he had operated successfully on one of the junior members of the Royal family.'

'I see,' said Tyrrell. 'I have heard a little about his professional life, but I am also interested to know what he was like as a person.'

'He was very good looking, sir, and was one of those people who excelled at almost everything to which he turned his hand. There is no doubt from what Lady Elizabeth told me that he was a highly gifted surgeon, but he was also a sportsman, who got a blue for hockey at Oxford, and he had an uncanny skill as a woodworker, specializing in the making of miniature furniture. Lady Elizabeth's mother had been given an elaborate doll's house as a child before the war and she passed it across to her only daughter, who unfortunately failed to appreciate it. With the advent of the twin grandchildren, though, one a boy and the other a girl, Mr Kershaw set about repairing both it and some of the furniture as well as introducing many new pieces. He made a point of setting aside Sunday afternoons for the woodwork, with just a break for tea, unless Lady Elizabeth was there, when afterwards, if the weather was fine, they would take a walk, and if not, play a game of chess. Mr James had taught her to play when she was in her teens and I gather that she was quite accomplished at it.

'A number of Mr Kershaw's pieces have been exhibited at craft shows and won prizes. There are some photographs of them in a back number of one of the specialist magazines and I expect Lady Elizabeth would be able to find it for you if you would like to see it.'

'Yes,' Tyrrell said, 'I would be very interested in that. We have already been admiring the miniature dining room table up in the workshop, which he was obviously working on during the afternoon before he was killed. Would you say that the marriage of Lady Elizabeth and Mr Kersahw was a happy one?'

'I would prefer it, sir, if you were to ask her ladyship that question. You see, she would never have discussed her marriage with a servant, or anyone else. It would have been completely out of character for someone with her background to do so.'

'I understand that, but you must have gained some impression of their relationship.'

'The aristocracy, sir, and she is a member of it, have always had different standards to most other people. How shall I put it? They sometimes make accommodations that others do not. Would someone like her confide in or gossip with an ex-Barnado boy, whose background was unknown and who had been in service all his adult life? Of course she wouldn't and, equally, I would have been highly embarrassed had she tried. I know what you are going to say and that is that I must have noticed this and that over all these years. I can only say that if I did, I immediately put it out of my mind.'

'What about the younger son of the late Earl?'

'The Honourable James Brantley, sir? He had been a friend of Mr Richard since their time at university together and remained so. He is godfather to Mr Simon,

23

one of the twins. He often used to come here in Mr Michael's younger days, who always enjoys his visits, particularly when he got older. He also used to take both the children to pantomimes in the West End at Christmas time and was very generous with birthday presents.'

Tyrrell inclined his head. 'I gather from her entry in *Who's Who* that Lady Elizabeth is on the Board of Governors of a well-known girls' school and also occupies herself a great deal with church matters and a number of charities.'

'Indeed sir. Lad Elizabeth is a very industrious and busy lady.'

'Does she have secretarial help?'

'Her Ladyship uses one of the rooms upstairs as an office and a Miss Prodger comes in two morning a week to deal with the correspondence and e-mails.'

'Does Lady Elizabeth have a personal maid?'

'No, sir. She prefers to look after herself in that regard, although she does get the cleaning woman to bring down the sheets and pillowcases for me to put into the washing machine.'

Tyrrell nodded. 'Well, thank you, Parker, you've been most helpful. It's quite possible that we may need to talk to you again and I take it that you will be remaining here in service with Lady Elizabeth.'

'Yes, sir. Her Ladyship has already made it clear to me that that is her wish.'

'And no doubt you are quite happy with that?'

The man inclined his head slightly. 'Would that be all, sir?'

'Yes, for the moment, thank you. We may have a few

more questions when Mr Pocock has shown us the rest
of the house, and I take it that you will be available.'

'I shall be in either the kitchen or my sitting room,
sir.'

'Right. I'm sure you won't take it amiss if we glance
at your accommodation as well as everywhere else. We
won't need to disturb anything.'

'Very good, sir.'

The man rose from his seat and left the room, closing
the door behind himself almost silently.

'What an extraordinary relic from the past!' Sarah
said.

Tyrrell smiled. 'You'd be surprised how many of that
ilk are still around. You just have to know where to
look. Now, Jack, what have you got to show us?'

They started on the ground floor. There was a
surprisingly large cloakroom off the hall just inside the
front door, with an umbrella stand and coat rack just
inside and plenty of room for the set of golf clubs and
shoes, including Wellington boots. The dining room was
on the opposite side of the hall to the drawing room. It
contained a large table with eight chairs around it, a
sideboard, on which were standing a number of
decanters, and an open fireplace. There were prints on
the walls, including one of an Oxford college and a large
country house. Leading off it was a further room, which
was clearly Lady Elizabeth's office, containing filing
cabinets and a desk on which was a computer and
printer. Facing the back garden was a large kitchen
with an Aga against one wall, a sink at right angles to
it with a large refrigerator and freezer beside it and

there was a heavy wooden table in the middle of the floor. Parker's sitting room, which was through a door at the side, contained an easy chair, a small desk, a bookcase, a radio and TV set and a shower room, with a basin and a lavatory, which had been partitioned off on one side.

Upstairs, Lady Elizabeth used the master bedroom with en suite facilities, which was on one side of the first floor and there was a matching double spare room on the other, which contained a double bed and two cots. Kershaw's room, at the back of the house, was of modest size and he clearly used the adjacent fourth bedroom as a dressing room. The wardrobe contained his suits, all in immaculate order and the winter ones were in covers with tissue paper inside, and the chest of drawers contained underwear, socks and carefully folded and ironed shirts.

'Parker's work, no doubt,' Tyrrell said.

'Yes, sir,' Pocock replied. 'There is an iron and a board in one of the cupboards in the kitchen. Evidently, Mr Kershaw didn't like his shirts to be sent to the laundry and Parker also regularly pressed his suits and arranged for them to go to the dry cleaners when necessary.'

'And what arrangements does Lady Elizabeth make for her own laundry?'

'Parker said that she preferred to deal with that herself, although he did launder her sheets and pillow cases, which the cleaning woman brought down on a regular basis.'

'Where does Parker sleep?'

'He has the fifth bedroom, which has a basin in it

and, as you've already seen, he used the shower room downstairs near the kitchen.'

'Did Parker say if they often had visitors for the night?' Sarah asked.

'Apparently, ma'am, hardly ever in recent years. The grandchildren, though, do come from time to time to stay for a few days with their mother.'

Tyrrell nodded and looked towards his two assistants. 'I think that will suffice for the time being. I'd like you both to accompany me during my visit to Lady Elizabeth tomorrow and Mark, perhaps you'd also do some background work on Kershaw's professional career before you both go to the hospital.'

CHAPTER TWO

Tyrrell wasn't the least surprised to find that Kershaw's son had a substantial manor house near Hatfield in Hertfordshire, nor that Lady Elizabeth was supported by a Norland nanny, a maid and a cook in her task of looking after the two children. She was a tall, slim and elegant woman and was wearing a grey tailored suit. She was rather younger than Tyrrell had been expecting, looking to be no more than in her late forties or early fifties. She met them in the hall, gave each of them a brief handshake and then led them into the drawing room, which had bow windows giving a sight of the well manicured lawn and trees beyond.

'It's very good of you to see us at such short notice at such a sad time and you will no doubt have heard from Parker that my two assistants were with me at your house in London yesterday,' Tyrrell said. 'He told us how he found your husband lying at the base of the staircase leading to the loft in the garage, having died as the result of a serious head injury. Our forensic team are satisfied that it could not have been caused accidentally. We will be making enquiries at the hospital, but we wonder if you had any hint of his having received threats recently, perhaps in relation to his work.'

Lady Elizabeth had been sitting bolt upright in her chair, but there was no tension in her face as she looked at the detective unblinkingly.

'My husband liked to keep his professional life completely separate from the one he led at home, Chief Superintendent,' she said. 'He never discussed his patients with me and, by the same token, he did not wish to have social contacts with his colleagues. I have no idea how they viewed him and you would have to speak to someone at the hospital about that.'

'What about his domestic and social life in Highgate?'

'We led almost completely separate social lives once our twins, my son, who is married with two children, and my unmarried daughter, who works in London as a lawyer, left home. You may be wondering why someone in my social position should have married Richard. The short answer is that I had been completely bowled over by him from the first time I met him, having previously had the most ludicrously restrictive upbringing. I never went to school, having a private governess, and had virtually no experience of life at all until the age of eighteen, when my father, following pressure from my mother, decided to give a ball at his country seat in Surrey to celebrate my birthday. The partner, who had been arranged for me, was taken ill with acute appendicitis shortly beforehand and my younger brother, James, suggested that Richard would make an admirable substitute. The two of them had been friends at Oxford and after they came down, James to a job in the City and Richard to medical school in London, they kept in touch with one another.

'Knowing him to be excellent company and also good looking, James thought that I would get on well with him and that he would make an ideal partner for me. That's how we came to meet and our wedding followed later on, although that was not without its problems. My father and my stuffy elder brother, Rupert, didn't approve and for a time it looked as though, if we went ahead with it, I would be cut off from the family altogether.

'It was my mother, who was about the only person capable of getting round my father and did so with her usual efficiency, who saved the situation. She pointed out that they had to keep up with the times and that he would become a laughing stock if it became known that he had objected to a man with a first-class degree from Oxford, had just qualified in medicine and was already expected to make a name for himself in the profession. If the question of succession was worrying him, that was covered by my two elder brothers, one of whom already had children.

'My brother, James, was to be the best man and it was he who finally persuaded my father to accept the situation. Rupert, though, never did. He refused to come to the wedding and we haven't spoken to each other since. I haven't had any contact with his children or grandchildren, either, and I doubt if I ever will. Needless to say, he has made no effort to contact me since Richard's death. The very reverse has been true of James; he was the first person to get in touch with me after Richard's death. He didn't forget Parker, either, giving him a ring and offering him his condolences.

'I have always been extremely fond of James. He likes to give the impression that he is nothing but a lounge lizard, but he is on the board of a big finance company, is an expert in fine arts and is certainly no fool. He was very good to me when I was a child and lonely, and has been equally so ever since. It's not every older brother who, with infinite patience, would teach his much younger sister to play chess and various card games. I still see quite a lot of him and my life would be much duller without him.'

'And your own marriage proved to be a success?'

The woman raised her eyebrows slightly and, for a moment, Tyrrell thought she was about to produce some withering reply, but then the suspicion of a smile crossed her face.

'Richard was a very good father to our twins, who were born within a year of the marriage, especially during the family holidays. At home in Highgate, he constructed a tree house in the garden and also a flying fox and later on encouraged our son with games, playing tennis and golf with him. Unfortunately, our daughter, Alison, isn't and never has been interested in that sort of thing; she was always very quiet and self-contained as a child, liking to play on her own and has remained the same ever since. No doubt your men have shown you the dolls' house which had originally been made for my mother and which she gave to me. It had been in the loft and Alison used to spend hours up there, arranging and rearranging the furniture and making up stories about the people living in it and I rather hoped that we would be able to pass it across to her own children, if and when the time came, but that wasn't to be.

'Academically, Alison was much brighter than her twin brother and she went to a prestigious boarding school. I was not too keen on that idea at first, but both she and my husband were set on it. In due course she obtained a place at Bristol University and it was a great surprise to both of us and I have to admit some hurt, when, while there, she married a fellow student and we weren't invited to the wedding. The marriage was not a success, we never even met the young man, nor his parents, and she was divorced a year later. I can't see her ever getting married again. I used to worry about her a good deal, but now in her own way she seems happy enough, having become a partner in a firm of solicitors which specializes in divorce, but she seems to have very few friends.'

'Do you not see her at all?'

'Very occasionally I have lunch with her, when I am in central London and she is free, but she hardly ever comes out to Highgate. I do still worry about her, as did Richard, but we both learned to accept Alison as her own person. We always hoped that she would mellow as she got older and at least recently she accepted an invitation to a dinner in Highgate, which we gave for Richard's first assistant and his wife.

'Anyhow, with the advent of our granddaughter, Louise, Richard decided to refurbish the doll's house and make new furniture for it. The little girl is far too young for it at the moment and the work on it is sadly unfinished, but, even so, it should give her a great deal of pleasure in the future.

'I am not in a position to comment on Richard's

surgical skills, although his reputation speaks for itself, and there is no doubt at all that he was a genius in all sorts of ways with his hands. As for our private life, we understood each other perfectly and it's not every married couple who can say that. His life at the hospital was almost a closed book to me and you will have to ask his colleagues there about that.

'How, you are no doubt asking yourselves, am I able to discuss Richard in such a dispassionate way when he has met with such a horrible death only a few short days ago? Well, my maternal grandfather, who died before I was born, lost his leg in the first war and on his return is alleged to have said to my grandmother, who threw a fit of hysterics when she first saw him after it had happened: "Good God, woman, it's only a leg and if I'm able to accept it, so should you!"

'That may well be apocryphal, but I have seen photographs of him on his horse and also the splendid entry in the score book of the one of the annual cricket matches between the house and the village in which he is recorded as having been dismissed "stump before wicket."

'So I suppose you might say that I have inherited some genes for a phlegmatic temperament from my mother's side of the family. What am I going to do now? I will turn up at the memorial service that is bound to be held in the hospital chapel, I shall remember the happy times, of which there were many, and I will continue to help my children and grandchildren in any way I can.

'As far as the house in Highgate is concerned, I will have to make a decision about that in due course, but I am in no hurry to do so. I like it there, there is my charitable and other work and in due course, London will no doubt have its attractions for my grandchildren. As for Parker, he will remain in my employ for as long as he wishes. Since my early childhood, he has always been there for me and I have no intention of letting him down now. No doubt the time will come when he may want to retire, but he has already made it clear that he has no such plans at present.

'No, I haven't forgotten your original question. I don't know of anyone who might have wanted to harm Richard, if indeed his death wasn't an accident.'

'How about your husband's own family?' Sarah asked.

'Richard was, like Parker, an orphan, which is perhaps one of the reasons why the two of them got on so well together. He was adopted by a well-off, childless couple soon after his birth; both of them died when he was at university and they left him well provided for. As I understand it, he had a very happy childhood and adolescence.'

'You mentioned your daughter as being a solicitor. What does your son do?' Tyrrell asked.

'He works in the City. I'm afraid I don't know exactly in what way – corporate finance is not one of my interests. He got on very well with his father, despite the fact that he isn't good at ball games. He has always been a trier, though, and a cheerful one at that, which was very much to Richard's liking.'

'Was your husband such a stickler for punctuality as Parker indicated to us?'

The woman gave a hint of a smile. 'It would be

difficult to exaggerate it. If we were going somewhere, he would be pacing around ten minutes before we were due to leave and at times, I have to confess, I found it a bit wearing, particularly when our children were young.'

'How did Parker deal with that?'

'One of Parker's great skills is to adjust his attitude and behaviour to those he is serving. With Richard, he even used to outdo him in the punctuality stakes, but with me he is much more relaxed, pandering to my difficulty in getting going in the morning, and I have no doubt that he will continue to do so now.'

'I think it would be helpful if I were to have a chat to your brother, James, as he obviously knew your husband so well,' Tyrrell said. 'Would you be able to let me have his phone number so that I can fix a suitable time?'

Lady Elizabeth gave him the suspicion of a smile. 'That shouldn't be difficult, he lunches at his club every day and no doubt he'll ask you to join him. He's very hospitable is James. I'll get it for you right away.'

'What an extraordinary woman!' Sarah said on their way back to London.

'Yes, I agree,' Mark Sinclair said. 'Is she an eccentric aristocrat like some of those portrayed in books and television, or is her cool reaction to her husband's horrible death just an act? I incline towards the former. The odd female aristocrat has always kicked over the traces. One of the most remarkable of them was Jane Digby, about whom I read a fascinating book not that long ago. A member of a distinguished family, the things she got up to in Victorian times, dwarf anything we've heard today. Running away from a marriage to a much older man, affaires with all and sundry, an illegitimate child with the mad King Ludwig of Bavaria, whom she abandoned and finally living with a sheikh in the desert and fearlessly riding camels. You name it, she did it.'

'So you think that Lady Elizabeth might be in the same mould, Mark? Tyrrell said.

'Yes, I do, if not in quite the same dramatic fashion.'

'I'm not so sure. I think her cool manner was just her way of hiding her real feelings.'

Mark Sinclair and Sarah Prescott were able to obtain an appointment with Paul Maitland, the senior physician at St Gregory's Hospital for three o'clock that afternoon and met him in his room in the private consulting suite on the ground floor there.

The man, tall and good looking, had one of the purest heads of white hair that Sinclair had ever seen and he got up from the chair behind his desk as they were shown in and shook both of them warmly by the hand.

'Good to see you both,' he said. 'The first thing I would like to say is that if you have any difficulties here with anyone, medical or administrative, let me know and I will sort it out. I do have one favour to ask of you, though. There is a meeting of the medical staff committee at five o'clock this afternoon, I am expecting a full house and I'd like to introduce you to everyone. While not anticipating any great problems, they are more likely to be cooperative if they have faces to relate to, but inevitably there is the odd barrack-room lawyer who likes the sound of his or her voice.'

'That makes good sense to me,' Sinclair said. 'What do you think, Sarah?'

'I agree and it's likely to save us from having to make lengthy explanations each time we see a member of the staff. Our meeting with them is also bound to be talked about and may well help to reassure the junior medical and ancillary staff as well. Do you think that everyone will accept our presence without too many reservations, Dr Maitland?'

'I wouldn't go as far as to say everyone and, as I inferred, there are some nitpickers amongst the staff as a whole, but I have long experience in dealing with them and all you need do is let me know and I will deal with them,' he said with a smile. 'Any questions or observations of your own at this stage?'

'We are quite satisfied that Mr Kershaw was murdered,' Sinclair said, 'but that is not to imply that anyone in the hospital was involved, although at this stage we can't rule out that possibility. We have already started to make enquiries about Kershaw's domestic and private life away from here and there is also the possibility that a patient or relative of one had a grudge against him, but in any case, we would very much value your own view of him. You must have known him well and, imagine, may have had some influence over his appointment here in the first place.'

'You're quite right, I did. Firstly, let me say that I always had the greatest respect for Kershaw's surgical skills and I doubt if there is anyone, anywhere, and that includes the United States or Europe, who is a better neurosurgeon than he was in a purely technical sense.

37

However, there are many who felt that his unconventional approach to the management of patients left a lot to be desired.'

'In what way?'

'Kershaw took the view that he was not at all good at coping with patients and their relatives at a personal level, and felt that anxiety about that interfered with his surgical skills. He believed that it was in everyone's interests for that side of things in his cases to be handled by those who were temperamentally better suited to it, such as the referring physicians and, in particular, the neurologists. That attitude is not to everyone's liking, as you may imagine, but we do have three other neurosurgeons working here and if patients didn't like Kershaw's approach, they were always available as an alternative.

'It is always difficult to compare the performance of different surgeons in any discipline, but that is particularly true in the case of neurosurgery, as some areas of it carry greater risks than others. To be fair, his methods of selection were stricter than those of the others, but if one compares like with like, his results were better than any of them. I can't pretend to be a great connoisseur of surgical technique, but in my time I have watched a great many surgeons at work and in the past have assisted some of them, and I never came across his equal. He had great economy of movement, there never seemed to be much blood loss or crises of any consequence and he was phenomenally quick.'

'But surely,' Sarah said, 'if something did go wrong unexpectedly he would have had to explain the situation to relatives, wouldn't he?'

'You would think so, but it was part of the deal for that to be left to the referring physician or his first assistant, a man called Fielding.'

'Without knowing much about it, putting the onus on the shoulders of someone both junior to him and not directly responsible for the purely surgical side of things sounds very hard to me.'

Maitland nodded. 'There are a number of people here who would agree with you. However, Kershaw's training post provided the sort of experience that that of the other neurosurgeons does not. We have another surgeon here who takes responsibility for almost everything that happens on his firm. He interviews patients and relatives both before and after surgery, carries out a detailed physical examination himself and is both meticulous and very slow in the theatre. Neither his productivity nor his results are in the same league as Kershaw's were and his assistants get relatively little practical experience, particularly of the trickier surgical procedures. I was quite clear in my mind which of the two I would have chosen had I or a relative have needed brain or spinal surgery, and that was Richard Kershaw.'

'How did his current first assistant view things?'

'I never knew John Fielding to complain, but you would have to ask him yourselves. All I can say is that I always found him helpful, calm and efficient.'

'How about private patients?' Sarah asked.

'Kershaw didn't have any, not even the minor royal he operated on a few months ago – you may have read about it. She had an aneurysm on one of the arteries in the front of the brain and although she was in a private room here, he neither saw her pre- or postoperatively nor did he charge a fee. I was the physician involved and had to explain that although he was by some margin the best surgeon in the country for that particular problem, he had his own way of doing things and that there were no exceptions. I have to say that I was surprised that the powers that be agreed to his terms, so to speak, but they did and the result was an unqualified success. Despite his unusual approach, I fully expected a knighthood to follow, but we'll never know whether he would have accepted it if it had been offered.'

'What about records?'

'The important ones from Kershaw's point of view were kept by his ever efficient private secretary, who made copies of the hospital notes. She has an office in a nearby block of flats and she also kept in touch with those patients he had operated on either by post or telephone.'

'So she kept records in addition to those of the hospital?'

'Yes, she did. The hospital notes went on to the central computer system and she made her own ones for Kershaw's personal files, which he used for the number of important papers he wrote on surgical technique and outcome.'

'Was he popular as a colleague?'

'Only with those who were happy with his modus operandi.'

'Of whom you were obviously one,' Sinclair said.

The man smiled. 'You could say that.'

'How about the nursing and theatre staff?'

'He hardly ever went on to the wards, but the theatre staff were a different matter. He was a hard task-master, but they all respected him.'

'You mentioned his first assistant,' Sinclair said. 'What exactly did he do?'

'He was the one who usually opened the skull or spine and then assisted the maestro while he did the delicate bits. Fielding also had his own lists, which largely consisted of tumour biopsies, but to be fair, Kershaw did let him get on with some of the more important cases once he was happy with the man's level of skill. Fielding has been in the position for four years now and, in my opinion, should have obtained a consultant post long ago. He is an excellent all-rounder, being not only a first-rate surgeon, but also extremely good with the junior medical staff and nurses alike, not to mention the patients.

'Those who disliked Kershaw used to say that he was the one keeping Fielding back, so much did he depend on him, but I don't think that was fair. Fielding is a rather diffident fellow and doesn't fight his corner all that well. I, for one, would strongly support him as Kershaw's successor when the post is advertised, but I can't say that that would count in his favour all that much. I am too near retirement for that, although I still do have some influence.'

'The politics sound almost as devious as in our world,' Sinclair said. 'Is this man, Fielding, married?'

'I don't know. The only contact I've had with him has been purely to do with hospital business.'

'How much did Kershaw involve himself in the

hospital apart from the purely medical?' Sarah asked.

'As little as possible. He never attended the staff meetings and the only times I can remember his joining his colleagues in committee were those involving neurosurgical appointments, both senior and junior. Having said that, Kershaw did attract money, particularly for research and for the purchase of some of the latest equipment, which the Health Service baulked at, only offering support within the existing budget. Radiologists and pathologists as well as electrophysiologists have all benefited from his work and he never demanded that his name be put on their research papers, unlike many in his sort of position, particularly on the Continent. He was never the slightest bit interested in popularity, or in receiving fawning praise or respect.'

'How did women react to him?' Sarah asked.

The physician smiled. 'I am the wrong person to ask about that. Dynamic and successful men often seem to attract rumours concerned with that sort of thing and doubtless Kershaw was no exception. However, people know that I abhor gossip in any form and I am not averse to pointing that out, how shall I put it? Perhaps forcefully would be the best way.' The man looked at his watch. 'It's four-thirty now and, if you'll excuse me, I must go through the agenda of the coming meeting with one of the junior physicians, who is acting as secretary. Why not have a cup of tea in the canteen? My secretary will show you where it is and will collect you and show you to the boardroom in good time for the meeting, which is due to start at five.'

*

Their exposure to the committee was mercifully short and Sarah had to admire the way that Mark dealt with the one barbed comment that was directed at them. The meeting in the old boardroom was packed with a large number of the senior medical staff in several rows of chairs around the large table, with almost as many standing behind.

Maitland introduced the two detectives and expressed the wish that everyone should help them in every way so that their enquiries would be able to go as smoothly and as rapidly as possible. When the man asked if anyone had any specific questions to ask them, there were two, the first being about the length of time the enquiry might take and how they ought to react to press interest, which Sinclair answered clearly and concisely.

'It is impossible to predict time in a case like this right at the beginning of an enquiry and all I can say is that it is in everyone's interest for it to be as short as possible. I have little doubt that your chairman will brief you in detail about the press after my colleague and I have left the meeting.'

'Thank you, Inspector,' Maitland said. 'Just let me add that the senior administrator has already appointed a spokesperson to deal with that important issue and she will be covering it for you at the end of this meeting and making arrangements to communicate the same message to the rest of the staff, medical and lay. I will leave it at that, as I consider it essential that everyone should receive the same advice, which has already been agreed with the police. Anything to add, Inspector?'

'Only that you will no doubt see us on the premises during the next few days and please feel free to approach either of us if you have any specific concerns or questions.'

Maitland smiled at the two detectives. 'Thank you, Inspector. Are there any other points that members would like to raise before the detectives leave? Yes, Dr Westerby?'

From the chairman's tone of voice, it was only too obvious that the man who had raised his hand was one of those who always had some niggle or other, which he would bring up whatever the issue. He peered at them over the top of the lenses of his half-moon spectacles and tapped his notepad with his pencil.

'Is it really necessary for not one, but two detectives to come here and disrupt our work to look into a crime which, however dastardly, was committed many miles from here?'

Sinclair stared at the man for a few moments without blinking. 'The approach to one of the most senior officers at Scotland Yard, who himself directed us to come here, was made by the Chairperson of your health authority and if, as it seems, you are unhappy with the action taken, might I suggest that you take it up with her?'

An audible titter went round the assembled company and Maitland was clearly having considerable difficulty in keeping a straight face.

'That strikes me as being an admirable suggestion,' he said. 'Now, if there are no further questions or observations, it just remains for me to thank the inspectors for coming and to wish them well in their enquiries.

It had been the two detectives' experience that very often the head porter in hospitals like St Gregory's was the person who knew as much as anyone about the subtleties behind the façade, and so it proved. Unlike the somewhat frosty reaction of the senior administrator, a tense middle-aged woman, who seemed to have all the cares of the world on her shoulders, and whom they had met first thing the following morning, Benson, who like Parker, Lady Elizabeth's manservant, appeared to have no first name, but that was where the similarities ended. True, he was also slight and very neatly turned out, wearing a white shirt with a stiff collar under his immaculate grey suit and highly polished shoes. But there was nothing forbidding or formal about his manner, though, and he responded to their introduction with a warm smile.

'A terrible business this,' he said. 'Mr Kershaw will be sadly missed. I will give you both, sir and madam, every possible assistance.'

'Thank you,' Sinclair replied with a smile. 'For our part we will do everything we can to disrupt the routine of the hospital as little as possible. As a start, we would like to talk to Mr Kershaw's private secretary. I understand that she works in an office in the block of flats on the other side of the square.'

The man smiled. 'I was about to suggest the very same

thing, sir. Even though Miss Perry is not employed by the hospital, she knows as much if not more than anyone else about what goes on around here.'

'What do you suppose will happen to her now?'

'I believe, sir, that she will find other employment without undue difficulty. She has a formidable reputation.'

Armed with the number of Kershaw's flat, Sinclair pressed the button on the metal plate set into the wall by the entrance to the block.

'Miss Perry?'

'Yes.'

'Inspectors Sinclair and Prescott from Scotland Yard.'

'I'll let you both in, sir. The lift is on the right side of the lobby and the flat is on the fifth floor.'

The woman who opened the door of the flat looked to be in her fifties and could only be described as grey, from her faded hair down to her blouse, skirt, tights and shoes.

'This sad affair must have come as a great shock to you, Miss Perry,' Sinclair said, once the introductions had been made.

'Indeed it has, Inspector, and a responsibility.'

'Responsibility?'

'Yes. Mr Kershaw did very little private work, but he had no wish to rely on the NHS system for the notes he kept on the patients. He used to dictate them to me and I would enter them plus all the relevant investigation on to CDs. I sent hard copies of his operation notes to his NHS secretary and the original X-rays and contrast studies are held by the radiology department, with copies here. NHS notes are notorious for the frequency with which they are either misfiled, or go astray for other reasons, which is why I set this system up, with Mr Kershaw's enthusiastic support, of course. I have all our patients indexed by name with our own numbers and am able to access them both easily and rapidly.'

'I am most impressed. I understand that Mr Kershaw didn't carry out follow-up consultations himself.'

'That is correct, sir. Many patients were referred from outside London and I sent out letters to them plus stamped addressed envelopes every six months or so, depending on the type of surgery carried out, in order to find out how they were getting on. If necessary, the patients were seen by by Mr Fielding and the house officers in the hospital out-patient clinics.'

The flat was more spacious than the two detectives had expected. There was a good-sized lobby and, leading off it, a large living room, which acted as the office. In it was a substantial desk on which were three telephones, an internal hospital one, one connected to the hospital switchboard and an outside line. Miss Perry's computer was on the front of the desk, with a printer on a separate table beside it. In addition to the chair in front of the desk, there were two others by its side and the window gave a view of the square opposite the front of the hospital. The kitchen led off the living room and the bathroom and two bedrooms had separate doors in the lobby.

'You won't be able to get into the master bedroom, sir,' the woman said. 'It has a combination entry pad on it and I don't know the number. Mr Kershaw didn't want anyone apart from himself to have access to it, not even the cleaning lady.'

'Do you know why that was?'

'If you had known Mr Kershaw, sir, you would understand that any questions about his private life were completely off limits.'

'Did Mr Kershaw sleep here often?' Sarah asked.

'Yes, almost always if he was operating late and sometimes at weekends when he was working on the book on neurosurgery that he was writing.'

'What about the other small bedroom?'

'He used that as a library. It contains volumes on every aspect of the neurosciences including bound copies of the relevant journals and there is a large collection of reprints from other authors in the discipline. He also has his own word processor and internet connection in there.'

'So no one apart from Mr Kershaw slept here?'

'No, sir.'

'What are you planning to do now, Miss Perry?' Sinclair asked.

'That will depend on who succeeds Mr Kershaw. I like the work and it's possible that that person might wish to employ a private secretary and make use of the extensive records here. This flat, if redesigned, would make an excellent private consulting suite.'

'So Mr Kershaw didn't do private practice himself?' Sarah asked.

'No, he didn't.'

'Why was that?'

'That wasn't a question he ever discussed with me.'

'I gather that a Mr Fielding was Mr Kershaw's first assistant. Do you get on well with him?'

'Yes, I do. He is a very considerate and quietly spoken man, very different from the way Mr Kershaw was. There is no doubt that he is a very talented surgeon, too, but I doubt if he would be able to fight his corner in the hospital as effectively as Mr Kershaw did. If ever a man had a cutting edge, he did, and I think that was one of the reasons why we got on so well. He didn't tolerate what he termed inappropriate interference from either administrators or colleagues and neither do I.'

'Will you be continuing to work here for the time being?' Sinclair asked.

The woman nodded. 'I have already had a call from Lady Elizabeth, who has undertaken to cover my salary for another month while decisions are taken about all the data here.'

'I ask because one of our experts, a Mr Pocock, will be coming here later today with one of his assistants to look at all the rooms here in detail, included the locked one. It may take him some time, but I'm sure he'll inconvenience you as little as possible.'

'I look forward to meeting him.'

Sinclair glanced at his watch after they had left the flat. 'I'll give Miss Graves a ring as Tyrrell will want to have a meeting with Tredgold as soon as possible and then I thought I might see if I can get hold of this chap, Fielding. Would you like to join me?'

'I think I'll leave that to you. I promised I'd let Jack know when he could give the flat the once-over and then I have another idea. You remember Rebecca Cochrane, the daughter of the psychiatrist who was murdered last year?' Sinclair nodded. 'She was a senior registrar at this hospital at that time and I interviewed her at some length. If she's still here, she may well be a consultant by now and might be able to give me some more background on Kershaw.'

'Good idea.'

CHAPTER THREE

Sinclair found John Fielding in the office of Kershaw's ward having a chat to the sister in charge.

'I don't want to interrupt your work,' the detective said, after he had introduced himself, 'but I wonder if I might have a word with you when convenient?'

Fielding gave him the hint of a smile. 'As you may imagine, in view of what has happened, we're not as busy as usual. Why not now?' he said, then looked round at the sister, raising his eyebrows slightly.

'That's all right, Mr Fielding, I've got plenty to do on the ward. I expect you could each do with a cup of coffee.'

'That would be more than welcome, Sister. Thank you very much.'

The woman coloured slightly. 'That's all right, sir. I'll see to it right away.'

'The tragic death of Mr Kershaw must have come as a terrible shock to everyone at the hospital,' Sinclair said when the sister had left he room, 'and particularly to those in the neurosurgical department.'

'Yes, it was an appalling business.'

'How did you hear about it?'

'I was getting my notes up to date in Kershaw's office that Sunday afternoon and when I had finished, I rang his house in order to check the operating list for the following day with him and to confirm that Corson, the anaesthetist, had been fully briefed. It must have been about six o'clock and it was his manservant, Parker, who answered and told me that he had found Kershaw dead in the garage and that the police were there. I was shaken to the core and decided to telephone Dr Maitland, the Chairman of the Medical Committee, immediately to let him know what Parker had told me.'

'How did he react?'

'He just thanked me and said that he would deal with matters at this end.'

'Did you ring your wife, too?'

'No, I thought it would be better to tell her face to face. After all, she had met Kershaw for the first time only a few weeks ago when he invited us both to dinner and I knew how upset she would be. You see, at the dinner, he took a lot of trouble to put Annette at her ease and she told me on the way home what an attractive personality he had. When I did tell her, she was naturally very upset and also worried, as I am, about our future in the light of what has occurred.'

'What is going to happen to this unit?'

'Dr Wentworth came back to me and said that I should carry on with the few operations that couldn't be delayed and do my best to fight off the administrators, one of whom had already poked her nose in. She was spouting the usual mantra about healthy and safety and wanting to close the ward down completely.'

'How did you cope with that?'

The man allowed the hint of a smile to flit across his face. 'I asked her what was safe about delaying surgery on a man's spine, which if it were left, would lead to permanent paralysis, or about allowing a woman to lose her sight if pressure on her optic pathways was not relieved by a comparatively straightforward operation. I'm pleased to say that both patients have done well, but since then, I have confined my activities to dealing with any queries that Miss Perry has been unable to handle herself. As you might imagine, that is no easy task. I have not operated again since, and the other neurosurgical firms are dealing with all emergencies. It's not that I don't feel competent to cope with the work, but there are always hazards in any branch of surgery, not least that on the brain and spinal cord, and in these litigious days, I thought it best not to take the risk.

'Maitland has continued to be very helpful and has made a point of having a chat to me most days, which I have found very reassuring.'

'I see. What do you think this is going to do for your future in neurosurgery?'

'Naturally, I am very concerned about that and Maitland has given me advice about that, too. He told me that neurosurgical services in the hospital as a whole would have to be reviewed, but in his opinion this hospital would be lucky to have me on the staff. However, he did point out that I must know that relationship between the various neurosurgical firms here were not the happiest and that already there had been jockeying for position. He told me that he happened to know that a retirement on health grounds was about to take place at an excellent unit outside London and that perhaps it would be wise to look into that even before it was advertised. He said with a smile that he was not without influence here and he felt that the other neurosurgeons would also support my application should the idea commend itself to me.'

'And would it?'

'Very much so, in view of what has happened here.'

'How do you suppose your wife would view a move out of London?'

'Annette was telling me only a little time back that she doesn't like the atmosphere here and that she hadn't mentioned it to me before because she didn't want to prejudice my career in any way. She pointed out that there was no real social life associated with this hospital and I've been so busy that we've never been able to make friends with the people who live close to us. There is also the question of us starting a family, which Annette is keen to do, but not with my being at Kershaw's beck and call the whole time. She was quite right, of course, and a new start away from London with fewer pressures, social and professional, might well be in both our interests.

'I am well aware that for some time she has been lonely and at something of a loose end and that was why I pulled a few strings to get a training post for her as a technician in the department of clinical neurophysiology here. I was very much helped by a friend of mine, Rebecca Cochrane, who was a student here with me, and has recently been appointed as a consultant in the department of cardiology.'

'And is your wife's new job working out all right?'

'Yes, it is, very well. Once the others in the department discovered that she wasn't going to pull a "high and mighty" act as the wife of Kershaw's first assistant and that she was prepared to be helpful to all and sundry, she was accepted without any reservations. She has risen to the challenge of getting on top of the bookwork and the practical aspects of the job and she's a different person as a result.'

'Did she ever meet Kershaw apart from at that dinner you mentioned?'

'No, she didn't and I have to say that it was one of the most excruciating evenings I have ever experienced as I am so hopeless with small talk. It's true that Kershaw did his best to make us welcome, but with his wife being stiff and formal, his daughter obviously shy and withdrawn and having very little to say, and Lady Elizabeth's brother telling awful jokes, I don't think I have ever spent a more miserable evening. I was well aware that my future very much depended on Kershaw's good will and there was I putting my foot in it by being stiff and tongue-tied.

'I had to take my hat off to Annette, though; she was brilliant. She was charming to Kershaw and was obviously not overawed by either Lady Elizabeth or her creepy manservant, the obsequious Parker. When we were drinking our coffee in the drawing room, Kershaw's daughter must have realized how embarrassed I was, because she looked across at her father and said: "Why don't I show Mr Fielding your workshop, unless of course you'd prefer to do it yourself? We've been talking about the relationship of surgery to art and I know he'd be interested." In fact, we hadn't been doing anything of the sort, but I'm sure that she realized that I had been extremely uncomfortable throughout the evening and that that might be a way out. Kershaw gave us a smile and said: "By all means, my dear, carry on. I'm far too comfortable here and enjoying interesting conversation, for once having nothing to do with medicine, to want to interrupt it." He then turned towards Annette and said: "In any case, my dear, I can't imagine you'd want to risk climbing steep steps in those elegant shoes of yours, which I have been admiring."

'He certainly had a point and I had told her before we left home that she oughtn't to wear ridiculously high heels as the Kershaws might have parquet flooring. Annette wouldn't have anything of that and asked me that if I wanted her to create a good impression, how could she possibly go looking dowdy?'

'How did Lady Elizabeth react to the suggestion of a visit to the workshop?'

'Merely with a stately nod and saying: "What a good idea!" '

'Were you impressed by what you saw up there?'

'I didn't really want to go, but I felt I had no alternative but to accede to the suggestion and I'm very glad that I did. I had no idea that Kershaw did work like that which I saw up there. The miniature mahogany table he was currently working on was particularly striking. Of course, I was well aware that the man was a genius with his hands in the operating theatre, his precision and economy of movement being quite remarkable.

'For the first time that evening, I really enjoyed

myself. To my surprise, I found Kershaw's daughter to be an engaging and knowledgeable companion. I was a bit concerned about leaving Annette behind, but I need not have worried; she had obviously enjoyed the whole evening and continued to do so, no doubt because Kershaw went to so much trouble to put her at her ease.'

'Did Kershaw mention the dinner to you afterwards?'

'No, thank God. I did write what I hoped was a suitable letter to Lady Elizabeth, but I'm not exactly versed in that sort of thing and I doubt if my feeble efforts went down particularly well as it must have been glaringly obvious to her how embarrassed I had been by most of the evening.'

'Did your wife make any comment to you about it later on?'

'She just told me on the way back home that she realized that I had been embarrassed by it, but that I took life too seriously and that I should have done what she did, relaxed and enjoyed it.'

'And do you think she did?'

'Oh, yes. She really sparkled that evening. Perhaps the unaccustomed wine had something to do with both that and what happened when we got home. I'll leave that to your imagination. It also made me realize that most of our problems with our marriage were related to my being selfishly obsessed with my work and that I should seriously consider getting a consultant post away from London, take more time off and perhaps then we might even agree to starting a family.'

Lady Elizabeth's younger brother, the Honourable James Brantley, came bustling into the front hall of his club in Pall Mall after Tyrrell had given his name to the porter. He was a great deal shorter than his sister and whereas she was pale, slim and elegant, he was tubby, almost completely bald and with a florid complexion. When he laughed, which he did frequently, his eyes almost disappeared behind his chubby cheeks.

'Welcome, my dear fellow,' he said when the introductions had been made. 'The Club has quite a decent sherry, so why don't we go into the small room off the library and have a glass or two before lunch. We won't be disturbed there.'

While they waited for the steward to appear, Brantley showed him round the library, then, once the decanter had been brought in, he looked intently at the detective across the table in the anteroom.

'Now, no doubt you want to know about all the family secrets?'

'It's really Richard Kershaw I'm most interested in.'

'In what way, exactly?'

'I understand that you were at Oxford together and I was wondering how he came to marry your sister. After all, he wasn't exactly to the manor born.'

'Well, you could say that I was responsible for that. You see, my father was persuaded by my mother that he should give a ball for Elizabeth's eighteenth birthday. Had you known my sister at the time, or even now, for that matter, you would have thought, as I did, that it was the last thing she would have wanted. However, because of her upbringing, Elizabeth clearly had no idea how to go against her parents' wishes, and maybe the idea was something of a guilt thing on the part of my mother at the way Elizabeth had been treated and she thought that a really grand event would be some recompense.

'You see, Elizabeth had been entirely educated at home by a string of governesses. It all started when she contracted rheumatic fever as a small child and she was labelled, quite unjustifiably as it turned out, as being delicate and having a weak heart. Weak heart, my foot! You should have seen the games we used to play in the garden when no one was looking, simple things like tag and running and hopping races. I had also taught her to play draughts and chess, and when it was wet, we'd settle down to that as well as card games and doing jigsaws together. She was good fun when she was on her own and I enjoyed her company, as I hope she did mine.

'The fact that she was treated as a semi-invalid was all the fault of the fussy old fool of a cardiologist, who was called in by the GP and found a cardiac murmur, at least he said he had. You see, much later on, when she was investigated properly, no trace of it was found. Maybe in his day he was competent enough, but after he had treated one of the Royals, he was given a life peerage and that's how he came to meet my father in the Lords. He became a political doctor and was way past it from a clinical point of view by the time he came to see Elizabeth. That, of course, was long before the House of Lords was emasculated and most of the hereditary peers were kicked out.

'Anyway, my father was persuaded that people would talk if nothing was done for his only daughter's eighteenth birthday and agreed to organize a dinner and a ball for her. A "safe" escort was found for her, but the man in question went down with appendicitis a mere fortnight before the event and when I was asked to find a suitable substitute, who wouldn't take umbrage at the last minute invitation, that's when the trouble started. Richard had been a friend of mine at Oxford and when we went down, we kept in close touch. He had got a first in his finals, had just qualified in medicine and was due to start his house jobs at St Gregory's in the autumn. Apart from his academic distinction, he was extremely good looking and also, when he tried, had exquisite manners and to cap it all, he was both available and up for it when I made the suggestion. He had to be vetted, of course, but Richard knew how to handle my father, who turned out to be putty in his hands.' Brantley raised his eyebrows and smiled. 'To be thoroughly vulgar, Richard filled the gap that evening in more ways than one and yes, you've guessed it, he got Elizabeth pregnant and, what's more, with twins. Despite that, she managed to hide her condition until it was far too late to do anything about it and marriage to Richard was the outcome.

'The whole business was too much for my father, William, and a few weeks before the twins were born, he died as the result of a heart attack. In fact, he had always had problems over Elizabeth.'

'What sort of problems?' Tyrrell asked.

Brantley raised his eyebrows slightly. 'You're no doubt familiar with the expression "an heir and a spare"?'

'So you think that your mother took advantage of that convention?'

'That's one way of putting it, but I hardly think it was planned. Elizabeth appeared when I was thirteen, she is slim and a good four inches taller than I am and even a bit more than that as far as my elder brother is concerned. She is athletic and still good at tennis, whereas the two of us could just about stagger round the croquet lawn on a good day. It doesn't take a geneticist to see the implications of that, although I have to admit that that it is all surmise on my part. It is not something that any member of my family has even hinted at, at least not in my hearing, and, having met my sister, you will know that she is not the sort of person to be tackled head on about anything, let alone something like that.'

'And what was your father's reaction to the events you described?'

'He was already unwell when he found out about the pregnancy and refused to have anything more to do with Elizabeth, but at least he didn't turn her out of the house, and died from a heart attack not long afterwards. In any case, there had been a distinct lack of warmth between him and my mother after Elizabeth's birth and perhaps that had something to do with his own indiscretions; he might well have had "*une petite amie*" hidden away in London when he came up for attendance at the House of Lords. Anyway, perhaps because he was also beginning to lose his marbles, he gave in over the wedding, which is more than can be said of my brother, who would have nothing to do with it and refused to attend the ceremony. It was also entirely due to my mother that Parker went into service with Elizabeth soon after the arrangement over the house in Highgate was made.

'The fact that my mother cut herself off completely

from Elizabeth after the wedding and later from her grandchildren as well, was probably the responsibility of my elder brother, the present Marquis. I wouldn't be surprised if her residence in the dower house on the estate and being kept in the manner to which she was accustomed, was conditional on her behaving in a way that that pompous fool thought would be appropriate.'

'And she's still there?'

'Yes, she is.'

'If you are correct about the circumstances of your sister's birth, what about her real father?'

'What I have already told you is pure speculation and I have no idea if Elizabeth has ever jumped to the same conclusions about her parentage as I have. Certainly, his identity has never been revealed and I wouldn't be surprised if my mother didn't know it either. That has happened often enough and, who knows, perhaps drink or even drugs had something to do with it. All I can say is that the man in question must have been both taller and a great deal more intelligent than the rest of the family. Elizabeth is as sharp as a needle and so, indeed, is her own daughter.'

'Did Richard Kershaw ever say anything about such speculations to you?'

'No. In the interests of keeping up my friendship with Richard and Elizabeth and also reasonable relations with my mother, whom I visit from time to time, I have thought it politic never to ask any of them about it all directly, nor to try to find out about it in other ways.'

'Why do you suppose that Kershaw agreed to the arrangement you've just described?'

'He didn't come out of it at all badly. After all, he and

his wife had a detached and attractive property in an agreeable part of London, he was relatively well off and, don't get me wrong, Elizabeth had her attractions. She may not be ravishingly beautiful, but she is a fine-looking woman all right and very intelligent, too. With that and her connections he was surely on a good wicket.'

Tyrrell nodded. 'What can you tell me about Parker?'

'Not a lot. He's what one might term a fader into the background, but he and Richard could hardly have been more different. It's possible that my brother hoped that he would be a constant irritant to Richard with his obsequious ways and the fact that with Elizabeth being so fond of him, he might act as a wedge between husband and wife. If so, he was mistaken. Maybe there were tensions to start with, but from what Elizabeth has said and what I observed myself, latterly the two of them got on splendidly. I have no doubt Richard finally revelled in the situation; who wouldn't, being provided with suits with knife-edge creases in his trousers and mirror-like polish on his shoes?'

'You have obviously kept in touch with Kershaw and your sister. Did you go to their house often?'

'Indeed I did. I am a godfather to their son and still keep in touch with him, his sister and my great niece and nephew. It may seem odd coming from a confirmed bachelor, some would even say sinister, but I am fond of children and I like to think that they feel the same about me.'

'How about the relationship of Richard Kershaw and your sister? You obviously must have seen a good deal of them together.'

'I'm quite sure that they both liked and respected each other and over the years developed a relationship with which they were both comfortable. In their different ways, they led full and successful lives and made such accommodations towards one another as were necessary.'

'And you sister's reaction to the tragedy of Kershaw's death?'

'Elizabeth doesn't and never has worn her heart on her sleeve and who knows what goes on behind the controlled and some would say icy façade of hers.'

'And their children?'

'Simon, their son, is charming, outgoing and very much the family man, not over bright, to be honest, but he is reliable, personable and people like that get on well in big corporations, particularly if there is a title or two in the background. As for Alison, their daughter, she has always struck me as being rather a sad person. She is divorced, seems to have few friends and her life seems to be her career and not a great deal else. In some ways, she's quite like Richard, being very focused on her work, but what she lacks completely are his charm and general *joie de vivre*, which he had in spades, and one might go as far as say that she is antisocial. I was going to say that she was rather like Elizabeth in that regard, but that isn't entirely true; my sister is able to lay on the social graces when she has to.

'It is also striking how much Alison lacks her father's. physical energy. When she was a child, Richard tried to get her interested in games, particularly tennis at which he was extremely good, and he even took my sister and the children on a skiing holiday. I gathered from Elizabeth that it was only a qualified success. Needless to say, Richard was an expert and Simon, although he had little aptitude for it, threw himself into it with enthusiasm, as he does with everything else. As for Elizabeth, she confined her activities to some decorous skating. Evidently, Alison proved a great disappointment to Richard on that holiday. She did make a start at skiing, but hated it and after a few days abandoned it completely and spent her time reading and occasionally going for walks with her mother and watching her skate.

'Remembering how ignorant Elizabeth had been about sex, I asked her one day what she had done concerning education with regard to her children.'

'And what was her reply?'

'She was profoundly embarrassed by the question, but did tell me that as she lacked the competence to do it and that Richard felt uncomfortable with it as well, they had decided to leave it to their respective schools, both of which she had been assured made adequate provision in that regard. Obviously, that side of things has worked out well for Simon; you only have to see him with Louise to know that. I did worry about it with Alison, though. She has always seemed such an unhappy person, but I have felt all along that it would be inappropriate for me to interfere.'

'What does your niece do?'

'She's a solicitor specializing in divorce. You might think that a person, who never says much in company and lacks charisma, might have problems in court, but she doesn't. Out of interest, I attended one of the cases in which she was appearing and she was surprisingly effective. Unlike the other woman appearing for the wife, who was strident and showy, Alison had absolutely all the facts at her fingertips, quietly destroyed the wife's contention that her husband was being totally unreasonable and undermined her case to such an extent that it collapsed.'

'How did she get on with her father as an adult?'

'Much the same as she got on with everyone else, male or female: politely, but without ever letting her guard down. Richard was obviously concerned about her in the sense that he couldn't understand how anyone could lead such a boring life with seemingly no friends away from her work apart from her cat!'

'What's your view of her?'

'I believe he was quite wrong about her. Richard seemed incapable of understanding that there were plenty of people like her who didn't sparkle, want excitement, exotic holidays, or dramatic sex in their lives and were perfectly content with what they did have.'

'Does that imply that Richard Kershaw went in for all those things?'

'I have no knowledge of the sex thing. Neither Elizabeth nor he ever hinted at, let alone discussed that with me, but it was obvious that Richard had a type of life force, which is difficult to describe, but was only too evident when one was with him. He loved sport and taking physical risks such as when he went skiing and rock climbing with old university friends and he certainly lit up when in the company of attractive females.'

'How did your sister deal with that?'

'I believe that she wasn't interested in any of that sort of thing herself and had long since decided that the best way of coping with it was to turn a blind eye.'

'Any idea who might have wanted to harm Richard, let alone kill him?' Tyrrell asked.

'No, I haven't, but for what it's worth, my advice to you would be "*cherchez la femme*" and quite possibly la femme's husband. I suppose a disgruntled patient or one of their relatives are other possibilities.'

'Well, thank you for your comments. They've been most helpful,' Tyrrell said.

'Think nothing of it. If there is anything further you want to discuss with me, you will usually be able to find me here. Now, lunch awaits us, so why don't we go into the dining room? I expect you could do with a break from murders and other forms of skullduggery.'

Although Tyrrell's first impression of Brantley had been that he was no more than a self-indulgent lounge lizard, he soon discovered over lunch that that was far from the truth. After Oxford, the man had studied fine arts in Rome, Florence and Venice and was frequently called in by museums and auction houses for opinions about authenticity and advice about exhibitions. That hour and a half proved to be both extremely entertaining and instructive and the meal was excellent.

Sarah Prescott was able to arrange a lunch date with Rebecca Cochrane that same afternoon when she gave her a call at the hospital on her mobile.

'I would prefer somewhere well away from this place,' the young woman said. 'There is a pub about half a mile away from the hospital, which is never used by the staff, and I think that would be the best place. The clientele and the area may be a bit rough, but the food is perfectly reasonable. To save you having to hang about – there are some distinctly unsavoury characters wandering about there – I'll get there in good time and will bag a table.'

Sarah couldn't imagine why the young woman was so anxious about the locality. As a WPC, she had worked on the vice squad and it was immediately obvious to her that although the pub was in a rather run-down area, it was hardly the sort of place where drug dealers, prostitutes and their minders would be hanging around, let alone at that time of day. In the event, Rebecca was waiting for her on her arrival at a table in a dark corner, and those standing at the bar were not in the least threatening, obviously being mostly workers from the large building site across the road.

'Good to see you again,' Rebecca Cochrane said. 'Sorry to have made such a performance of meeting you, but I wouldn't be surprised if lots of people at the hospital already know who you are and, if we are seen together, the rumours are bound to start. I seem to attract gossip and in no time at all I might well be labelled as having something to do with Kershaw's murder, or even having been one of his mistresses. No, I'm not exaggerating,' she said, as she saw the slight raising of Sarah's eyebrows.

'I see. Well, I'm sure you haven't got much time to spare, so perhaps you'd tell me about Kershaw.'

'He was a typical alpha male, but there is no doubt at all that he was a quite brilliant surgeon in a purely technical sense, but that's where it ended. I don't believe he gave a single thought to patients as people – they were merely interesting cases as far as he was concerned. Don't get me wrong, his results were far superior to those of his colleagues and his phenomenal dexterity and speed in the operating theatre had a lot to do with that.'

'I've already heard that he left the patient management side to his first assistant.'

The young woman nodded. 'Yes, and that was one of the things that concerned me about Fielding as a friend and colleague.'

'You mean that he was being exploited?'

'Yes, that was part of it, but I wouldn't want to give you the impression that John Fielding was Kershaw's poodle. In my view, he's bound to become a very successful consultant neurosurgeon in the very near future and already has had a great deal more hands-on experience than the usual candidates for such a post. I've never heard him complain about his lot, either. No, the person I'm most concerned about is his wife, Annette.'

'In what way?'

'They've been married for about three years and, apart from attending the wedding – John and I were students here together – I hardly knew her until she obtained a job at the hospital as a trainee technician in the department of clinical neurophysiology.'

'Yes,' Sarah said. 'I learned something about the subspeciality from your father's friend, Walter Paterson, whom I met at the Henshaw Hospital when we were investigating your father's death last year.'

'Well, in that case, you'll probably be aware that a whole variety of tests are done on patients in that department, some quite complex, and as I discovered that Annette had very little background in science or medicine, she must have had powerful backing to have got in.'

'Her husband?'

'No, he doesn't carry enough clout. I'm pretty sure that Kershaw was involved.'

'Are you suggesting that he had some ulterior motive?'

'Yes, just that. Why else should he have started to take an interest in that sort of test on his patients, when, as far as I know, he never had before? He was more than a bit interested in that young woman, too. They may have thought that they managed to hide it, but you can usually tell if you know what to look for and she has a nice line in blushes.'

'So you think that she wasn't exactly upset by his attentions?'

'More than that, I reckon, seeing the way in which she reacted.'

'Do you suppose that her husband noticed anything?'

'Who knows what goes through the mind of someone who has always seemed to me to be totally bound up in his career?'

'How well do you know John Fielding?'

'We were contemporaries as students here. He was always totally obsessed with medicine and, in particular, surgery and that's why I was so surprised when he got married. As far as I know, and students in the same year, which we were, always know who is going out with whom and I'm almost certain that he never did so with any of us at that time, male or female, and the same was true of the nurses.'

'What is his wife's background?'

'I believe that her father's a retired judge, but I have no idea what if any jobs she did before she got married, but whatever they were, at her age, she's only twenty-two, it couldn't have amounted to all that much because she went to university on leaving school. I reckon that getting married to a trainee neurosurgeon, let alone one working with Kershaw, was about as unwise as one could get for a person like her. It seems to me that John is always at the hospital, even most weekends and quite a few nights as well when his firm is on call for emergencies.'

'Have you heard any gossip from your colleagues about Kershaw's death?'

'I'm afraid I can't help there. I do attend as many staff meetings as I can, but I can't stand tittle-tattle and that's not exactly a secret.'

'Any view yourself?'

'Not really, although with Kershaw's reputation, I would have thought that an angry husband or partner of one of his girlfriends might be a possibility.' The woman looked up and stared at Sarah across the table for a moment. 'That remark's not based on any evidence and I shouldn't have made it.'

Sarah nodded. 'No need to worry, it won't go any further. From what I've heard already, though, this hospital doesn't sound as if it's a particularly happy place to work in.'

'It's not, specially for the students. In my father's day,

71

they were predominantly male and St Gregory's had its own medical school and there was much more camaraderie then than there is now. A short time before I came here as a student, the medical school joined up with those from two other former independent teaching hospitals and, as a result, the students don't belong in the same way as they used to. There are many who think that is a good thing, but I'm not so sure. The importance of games has also diminished very considerably and they were undoubtedly a useful outlet for testosterone-driven young men. Now, it's all about relationships and living in shambolic mixed flats.'

Although they continued to chat about the hospital for most of their meal, Sarah learned nothing of any real substance about Kershaw, but she was still convinced that Rebecca Cochrane was both worried and holding something back. She decided, though, not to press her for the time being and at least she had got a clear idea of the organization of the hospital and some of the tensions existing between the members of the staff.

CHAPTER FOUR

The two detectives met Tyrrell in his office early the following morning and gave him an account of their meetings with John Fielding and Rebecca Cochrane.

'So, Sarah, you think that Rebecca is both gay and is more than a bit interested in the wife of Kershaw's first assistant?'

'Yes, I do, sir. I suspected she was the former when we were investigating the murder of her father and now I'm sure of it. Why else would she be so concerned about Annette Fielding being neglected by her husband? To add a bit more spice to it, Kershaw clearly helped the young woman to get her a job in the applied electrophysiology department, in which she is a trainee technician.'

'The implication being that Kershaw and the young woman were getting together in other ways as well?'

Sarah nodded. 'I also got the strong impression that Rebecca also suspected just that and that she was extremely upset by it.'

'And what about John Fielding, Mark?'

'I thought he was extremely impressive. He was quite frank about the difficulties of working for Kershaw, who was obviously a slave driver, but had nothing but praise for the man's skill as a neurosurgeon. He admitted that the job had taken over his life to a degree that was making him worried about his relationship with his wife, but the post she had obtained at the hospital in clinical electrophysiology had helped a great deal and, following that, she had become much more her old self. He also gave a graphic account of the one time Kershaw had invited them to his house for dinner not all that long ago. It appears to have been excruciatingly embarrassing, particularly for Fielding, with Kershaw being distinctly solicitous towards Annette, his daughter, Alison, being uncommunicative and Lady Elizabeth attempting to act the gracious hostess, but without conspicuous success. Her brother was also there and seems to have been the one person to have tried to stimulate general conversation, but without much luck, either. Alison, though, obviously decided that enough was enough and managed to get Fielding out of the drawing room after the meal by offering to show him Kershaw's workshop.'

'Right, thank you, Mark. Now, I'd like you to have a preliminary look at the locked rooms in Kershaw's flat and I propose to do a bit more research into Kershaw's family and I will need your help, Sarah, when I go to see Lady Elizabeth. Finally, would one of you make an appointment for all of us to see Tredgold as soon as possible?'

It took Tyrrell's secretary only a few minutes to find the address of Alison Stevens's rooms and to discover that she was due in court that afternoon, but that she was prepared to see him late that morning.

'She sounded rather abrupt, sir, although she wasn't exactly rude.'

'Don't take it to heart, June,' Tyrrell said with a smile. 'From what I've read about her in that divorce case that made the headlines recently, that seems to be her stock in trade, but thanks for the warning.'

After leaving his office, Tyrrell spent the rest of the morning in the records department with the help of the officer in charge, who looked up a number of items on the Internet for him, as well as some of their own documents.

The detective's first reaction on meeting Alison Stevens in her office just off the Strand was amazement that she could be the daughter of Lady Elizabeth, about whom he had heard so much from both Parker and James Brantley, and to whom he had spoken on the telephone. Unlike her mother, who had been softly spoken on the telephone, she was very direct, both in speech and manner.

'I hope this won't take long, Chief Superintendent,' she said after he had introduced himself. 'I have a very trying afternoon ahead of me.'

'I'll make it as short as I can,' he said, 'but I'm quite sure you realize that we have to talk to as many people as possible who knew your father well. There is also considerable pressure on us to make progress in the enquiry. Now, as a start, did you notice anything in your father's manner or appearance recently to suggest that he had been under any undue stress? I understand that you were at a dinner party that your mother gave for his first assistant, John Fielding, and his wife only a

few weeks ago. I'd be very interested to hear your
impression of that evening, in particular if there was
anything unusual about your father's behaviour then.'

'Father was at the head of the table and I was on one
side of him and Mrs Fielding on the other. Next to me
on the other side was the young woman's husband, my
father's first assistant. My father spent his whole time
flirting with her and it was only too obvious how
embarrassed the man was. My mother, who was on his
other side at the foot of the table, must have noticed it,
too – she would have had to be both blind and deaf not
to have done so – and did her best to talk to him.

'Such behaviour was by no means uncommon with
my father, but on that evening he was at his very worst
in that regard. Don't get me wrong, Annette, as she is
called, loved every minute of it and played up to it. My
uncle James did his best to lighten the situation,
particularly afterwards when we were having coffee in
the drawing room, but it didn't work and I could see
that Fielding was becoming more and more upset. It
was then that I had the idea of removing him from the
scene for a bit and suggested that he might be
interested to see father's workshop and some of his
woodwork in progress.'

'How did he and your mother react to that?'

'My father clearly guessed what I was up to and
milked the situation for all he was worth, making a
remark about Annette's very high heels being unsuited
to ladders and my mother was obviously relieved that
husband and wife were going to be separated. I thought
that taking Fielding up into the loft was going to be
something of an ordeal as he had seemed tongue-tied

during the dinner despite my mother's best efforts. I was quite wrong; he was obviously genuinely interested and amazed by my father's technical skill at woodwork, as indeed was I. I hadn't seen his latest effort, a mahogany dining table, before and it was beautifully crafted. We also talked a bit about his own career and he was unstinting in his praise of my father's surgical skills, too.'

'Did you at any time discuss what had happened that evening with your mother?'

'No. I haven't seen her on her own since that dinner party and, in any case, I didn't consider it my place to do so.'

'You never were married yourself, were you?'

There was a very long pause and then Alison lifted her head and stared at the detective for several moments and then said: 'What an extraordinary thing to say, Chief Superintendent. I think you'd better leave.'

'There is no record of your ever having been married, nor divorced and you also changed your name by deed poll between leaving university and joining the firm of solicitors. I have no doubt that you gave them an explanation that satisfied them.'

As Tyrrell watched her fiddling with the bracelet at her wrist, it was obvious that, for the first time since he had been with her, that she had completely lost her self-assurance.

'How did you find out?' she said after a long pause.

'Before meeting you, I decided to do some background research.'

'Does anyone in my family know anything about this?'

'I very much doubt it, and certainly not from either me or my assistants. May I ask why you did it?'

'To stop my father making snide remarks about my lack of boyfriends and insinuations that I was gay. As it happens, I'm not. I'm just not interested in that sort of thing with either men or women and having a Mrs in front of my name has proved to be a useful protection. Maybe I am this way because of the realization that there was something strange and unusual about my parents' relationship with one another. I can't remember ever having witnessed them showing signs of real affection such as embracing or kissing. It's true that my mother's attitude to both me and my brother, as children, was equally unemotional. She was attentive to our needs in the sense that she used to read to us and help with our schoolwork, but any physical contact was completely lacking. My father was the exact opposite; as young children, he was always hugging us, he tried to teach us ball games, took us swimming and there were treats such as visits to theme and safari parks, Madame Tussaud's, the zoo and so on. My mother never came with us. Recently, what has upset me greatly has been the fact that she is quite different with her two grandchildren.

'As I got older, I also began to notice how much my father lit up in the company of women and how they reacted to him in similar fashion. He was also the same with my Uncle James. There was always laughter when they were together and good-humoured banter. My father has never shown the slightest sign of disapproval at my lack of interest in physical activity, or, let's face it, my somewhat gloomy attitude to life. It

78

was as if he felt sorry for me. Inevitably, I reacted by becoming even more distant with both of them as time went by. Instead of understanding that my father and mother had totally different personalities and that they had adjusted to it by finding their own way of living amicably together, I just looked at it from a selfish point of view and, to put it frankly, I felt unloved. My father's unrestrained enthusiasm for physical activity and my mother's reticence were matters that I was incapable of dealing with and were the main reasons for my living apart from them as soon as I was able.

'When I left university, I decided to lead my life in a way that was satisfactory as far as I was concerned and if others thought it odd or unnatural, so be it. I did see my parents and my brother and his family from time to time, but that was all and I had every intention of being independent financially and emotionally and that is what I have achieved,

'Why, in that case, did I interfere when the Fieldings came to dinner? It was because I couldn't bear seeing him being humiliated by my father and that silly young wife of his.'

'You must, though, have given some thought to the question of who might have hated your father enough to have killed him in such a brutal fashion.'

'Yes, I have, and my guess is that he cuckolded the wrong husband, or that maybe a relative of a patient whose operation went wrong might have been responsible.'

'Fielding, perhaps?'

Alison Stevens shook her head. 'I think that very unlikely. In my work I have seen at first hand many angry spouses and some who have inflicted violence on the other, women as well as men, and, in my view, Fielding doesn't have that type of personality.'

'What is your brother's view of your family's situation?'

'My brother is one of those people who can't see wrong in anybody. He sails along with an aura of optimism and general good will to all. He clearly loves his wife dearly, a feeling which is reciprocated, his children are a delight to him and he likes his work. I used to think that it was just a faintly sickening act when we were adolescents, but it isn't; it's just the way he is. He's a bit like a younger version of my Uncle James without the intellect or worldly cynicism.'

'Well, thank you,' Tyrrell said. 'What you have told me gives me a lot of useful background and let me assure you that the confidential elements that you have outlined will remain that way unless there is some compelling reason to the contrary. I have already seen your mother and I did not get the impression that she bore your father any ill will recently, or in the past.'

'After the way he behaved towards her, that, if true, borders on the incomprehensible.'

'Did your Uncle James share your view of your father?'

'If you've met him, you must know that he didn't. The two of them had known each other since university and continued to enjoy each other's company. If and when you either see him for the first time or again, my advice to you would be to take everything he says with a large pinch of salt: he enjoys laying things on "with a trowel".

'As to my father, I'm not saying that he couldn't apply the charm if it was to his advantage to do so, particularly with the opposite sex, but underlying that he was both cynical and totally selfish, interested only in his work, his hobbies and ogling young women, if that dinner party was anything to go by, which I think it was.'

'I take it, then, that you won't be attending his funeral, or any memorial service at the hospital.'

'You take it correctly.'

'You seem to be implying that he was unfaithful to your mother. Have you any real evidence of that?'

'Had I been representing my mother in divorce proceedings, I guarantee that I would have found the evidence with the minimum of effort. As I was not representing her, I wanted nothing to do with it. Now, unless you have any further questions, I have work to do.'

'I do have one. May I ask what you were doing on the afternoon of the Sunday before last?'

The woman didn't seem in the least put out by the question and looked at Tyrrell intently before replying.

'I was working here. I had a case, which was coming up on the following day and I was putting the finishing touches to the strategy I was proposing to follow.' The woman stared at Tyrrell for a moment. 'And before you ask. I was alone, there were no phone calls and there is no one in a position to corroborate what I have just told you.'

'Right. Thank you. I won't disturb your morning any further, but I may possibly need to see you again.'

Tyrrell thought long and hard about his next step. Would he be justified in tackling Lady Elizabeth, or not? If, as seemed quite possible, her children were not Kershaw's, what point would there be in confronting her? It would only rake up old miseries for her and yet . . . and yet it might raise the barriers and she might be prepared to talk more freely about her husband. He was not looking forward to it, but he knew that however reluctant he was, he was going to have to do it and decided that it might help to have Sarah Prescott with him.

Lady Elizabeth was alone in the house in Hertforshire when the two detectives arrived, the nanny having taken the children to the local park, and the housekeeper had the afternoon off.

'I didn't expect to see you again so soon, Chief Superintendent,' she said when she opened the front door. 'How may I help you this time?'

'Believe me, I fully understand just how distressing all this must be for you, but there have been some developments which I feel I should discuss with you on your own?'

The woman's eyebrows went up slightly. 'Developments? What developments?'

'I saw your daughter this morning.'

'And?'

'Purely on her looks and manner, I found it difficult to believe that she was the daughter of you and Richard Kershaw. That raised the question of whether your husband was, in fact, her father, as there seems no doubt at all that you are her birth mother.'

'Someone, James perhaps, must have told you about this.'

'No, neither he nor anyone else gave me the slightest

hint about it.'

There was a long pause and then the woman nodded. 'Yes, I can believe what you said about James. He must have suspected, but under the façade of projecting himself as being nothing but a lounge lizard, he is in fact not only an able, but also an extremely nice man, quite unlike Rupert, my elder brother, the present Earl. I am, in fact, very grateful to James. It's not every older brother who would play games with a much younger sister, or indeed educate her. No, I'm not exaggerating; when I was old enough, he gave me books to read and then discussed them with me, making me think and develop opinions of my own. He taught me to play both draughts and chess, explaining that they were good training for thinking logically and being aware of the pitfalls of failing to analyze situations on the board, which would also stand me in good stead later in life. It was all done with a light touch and I really enjoyed those many sessions. I owe him a great deal and remain very fond of him. If it wasn't him who told you, may I ask what led you to the conclusion that Richard was not the father of my children?'

'It was purely the appearance and manner of your daughter. She is a great deal shorter than either you or your late husband, who, like you, was tall, good looking and well dressed. She is also rather overweight and clothes are clearly not one of her interests. As far as her manner is concerned, she is direct to the point of rudeness and also combative. None of these points would fit what I know of you, Lady Elizabeth, nor what I have learned about your late husband. It would, of course, be simple enough to prove it one way or the other by DNA testing.'

'Have you discussed any of this either with James, or anyone else?'

'No, I haven't and this is the first time that Inspector Prescott has heard my views about it, too.'

'And do you intend to share your opinions with anyone else?'

'Only with my other colleague, Inspector Sinclair, and I don't propose to bring the matter up with any member of your family, unless it proves to have some bearing on Richard Kershaw's death.'

'And what are your further views on that subject?'

'I have not yet had time to come to any informed conclusions. I need more information and am anxious to clarify matters, which is why I am here.'

'I see. Well, I was hoping that what happened was buried in the past, but as you have managed to get as close to the truth as you obviously have, then others may do so as well and I think the time has come to tell you about it, so that your colleagues or others don't leap to the wrong conclusions. Apart from the distress that that would cause me, it might act as a distraction from arriving at the truth about Richard's death, although I can't see what I am about to tell you could possibly have any bearing on it.

'As you no doubt have already realized, the whole matter came to a head after the ball for my eighteenth birthday. It would be difficult to exaggerate just how miserable my life had been up to that time. You have probably heard already that I had rheumatic fever when I was seven years old and according to the aged cardiologist, who came to see me, I had a heart murmur,

84

which meant that I was treated with the most ridiculous care. That meant no running about, no rough and tumbles, no games involving physical exertion, no riding and a dull and incompetent governess to look after my education.

'As I have already told you, had it not been for my brother, James, I might well have finished up "alone and palely loitering", if not confined to a bath chair.'

The woman immediately noticed the slight raising of Tyrrell's eyebrows and gave him a quizzical look.

'My apologies,' he said. 'I was just thinking, from what you've just said about her, that you would hardly have become familiar with Keats from your governess.'

Lady Elizabeth allowed herself a wintry smile. 'Indeed not; James again. I've already told you that he lent me books, some of which such as *The Joy of Sex*, would have sent my elder brother, a devotee of Opus Dei, into a towering rage and, given half a chance, he or my father would have thrown them all on to the fire. James also took me for drives, wearing a thick jumper and with a rug over my knees, but they only lasted until we were out of sight. We did all sorts of exciting things; we drove into London, he took me to London Zoo and even taught me to row on the lake in Regent's Park. "There," he said, after my first faltering strokes, "nothing wrong with you that escaping from that ghastly pap, which they seem to think passes as food, and regular exercise won't cure and I've always had ambitions to recline in the stern of a boat while being rowed by an attractive woman."

'I'm not saying that he managed to get me fighting fit, but instead of taking an improving book and sitting by the side of the lake in a deck chair, carried down, of course, by one of the footmen, usually Parker, I sneaked off and went for brisk walks. James knew perfectly well what I was doing during those all too frequent occasions and whenever we met, he would give me little, conspiratorial smiles. Parker was already well known to me, because he worked as a gardener's assistant when I was quite small and used to push me on the swing when no one was looking. He also helped me with the tiny allotment, which I was allowed to work on, provided, of course, that such exertion wasn't considered too strenuous.

'I don't know exactly why my father decided that a ball should be organized to mark my eighteenth birthday. Maybe he even felt a little guilty about my pseudo heart condition. You see, some eighteen months earlier, the family's new GP had overcome the fiction of it and the need for invalidism. He was convinced that there was nothing wrong with me and arranged for another cardiologist to see me in addition. Sophisticated tests were carried out at the National Heart Hospital and I was given a clean bill of health. Did anyone express sorrow about what had happened to me for all those years? No, they did not, except for James, who had a real go at my father.

'Anyway, the ball was arranged and I suppose that my father may have thought that this might be the opportunity to begin the task of getting me married off, no doubt egged on by my elder brother, who most certainly would not have relished the thought of having to be responsible for looking after me once my father died, which by then seemed imminent. Needless to say, it was not something I wanted, but my father never took my views into account, let alone over a matter which he considered to be within his province and nothing to do with me. Where did my mother come into all this? From the way she reacted to my father, and indeed to my elder brother, you'd think she was a non-entity, but she wasn't and the reason only became apparent to me when Richard pointed out the only too obvious differences between me and my father and two brothers. At least, that no doubt explained why they were so anxious to get me off their hands.

'When the man, a good ten years older than me and a distant cousin, who had been persuaded to be my partner, went down with acute appendicitis, I fondly hoped that I would be spared the ordeal of the ball, but all the arrangements had been made and James was given the task of finding an alternative.'

'And that was Richard Kershaw?'

'Yes. My father, as you may imagine, wasn't prepared to accept him just like that, particularly as he had only just qualified as a doctor, and he was duly invited to the house to be vetted. When he tried, Richard was able to charm the birds off the trees and he did just that with my father, such that the old man even suggested that the two of us might like to take a walk in the grounds, "to get to know each other!" I remember that for one fleeting second, for the first time in my life, I thought of rebelling and saying that I wasn't some pliant sheep waiting to be auctioned off like those at the country markets my father liked to attend, but the clandestine wink that Richard gave me put an end to that.

'Previously, I had never had the chance to let my hair

87

down and fool about other than with James, let alone with an attractive young man, who had nothing to do with the family. We played childish games like hide and seek, he pushed me to a prodigious height on the swing, which was suspended by ropes from one of the branches of a tree, and we had hopping races, which he let me win. And so I went to the ball and really enjoyed myself. I had had some dancing lessons, but never got on all that well with them, but with Richard it was quite different. He was a brilliant exponent of it himself and with him I felt relaxed, almost boneless and the champagne helped, too. Richard was the last to leave and gave me a goodnight kiss and ran his finger down my cheek as we stood for a moment on the porch, then he ran to his car, turned and waved. Then he was off, the car swerving madly on the gravel. I felt so happy and relaxed that I was even able to thank my father for organizing the evening and gave him a hug.

'I won't tell you what that vile man, who must have climbed up the drainpipe and got in through the window of my bedroom, which I had left half open, the evening being very warm and thundery, did to me that night. All I can say is that I never got over it and never will. He had a quite extraordinary smell, the memory of which remains with me to this day, neither will I ever forget his harsh voice as he told me that if I let out one single sound before he was well away, he would come back and kill me. And so I did wait, until through the window I saw him running away across the lawn.

'Physically, I wasn't badly hurt, but yes, I soon discovered that I was pregnant. There never was any question of a termination or the prophylactic use of the morning after pill; both my father and elder brother were members of Opus Dei, and I'm sure you know what that means – no contraception of any sort and the baby first, whatever the circumstances. There was never any chance of my escaping and going to a clinic, as I was kept a virtual prisoner in the house until it was far too late. And yes, it was two babies rather than one.

'It was Richard who told me that the man who had raped me, and who was a paranoid schizophrenic, had absconded from a mental hospital a few miles away and had hanged himself later that night in the woods a mile or so away from the house. My ordeal was kept firmly under wraps and as a result no hint of my rape reached the media. Richard assured me later that the risk of schizophrenia being passed on to the next generation was so low that it could be discounted. I later discovered that that wasn't quite the case, but by then it didn't matter, as neither of the twins showed the slightest sign of the condition and I have to say that that was a great relief to me.

'No doubt my brother, Rupert, had he spoken to me about the man who raped me, which he never did, would have said in his usual tactful way that I should pray for "the poor lost soul". The one thing he did do, with my father's agreement, was to persuade Richard to marry me before the pregnancy became too obvious.'

'Do you feel able to tell me how the family was able to persuade you and Richard Kershaw to go along with that course of action?'

There was a long pause and then the woman looked Tyrrell straight in the eye. 'Yes, I do, and the reason is that Richard was the one real friend I ever had and I miss him terribly and will continue to do so. You see, we understood each other completely and were able to accept our differences without any reservations. When we first met just before the ball, Richard's adoptive parents had died in a car accident some months earlier and they left him practically nothing, having lost all their money on stupid speculations. There was even a suggestion of a double suicide, as they hit a bridge on the M3 at high speed for no obvious reason and were killed instantly. Both of them were also well over the alcohol limit.

'Anyway, my brother Rupert and my father – I put it that way because my father had already had one heart attack, was frail and indeed died from a further one a few weeks later – came up with the following proposition. One of my father's houses, the one you've already seen in Highgate, would be made over to us and Parker would move with us, provided he agreed to the deal, although I doubt if he was given much choice. I had been left a substantial amount of money by my maternal aunt, who had no children of her own and she and her husband saw me as the daughter that they were unable to produce themselves. I used to stay with them from time to time and they provided the love and fun that my own mother never did. She came to the wedding on her own – she was a widow by then – and was charmed by Richard, as most women were. Sadly, she died soon after the twins were born and she left me all her estate, which was considerable. By then, my brother had already agreed that Richard would be given a generous allowance to enable us to live in appropriate style, provided he agreed to stick with me, until such time as he obtained a consultant post. Inevitably, that was going to take quite a long time, nearly ten years as it turned out.'

'And it all worked out pretty well for you?'

'Yes, it did, as I'm sure you have already concluded. Richard and I remained very good friends; he was such fun and he helped with the children more than I could reasonably have expected. Not only that, latterly, a lot of the charitable work I have been able to carry out was initially made possible by a few quiet words from him in the right places. I am quite sure that he would have liked a son of his own, one who was as dynamic, ambitious and as good at games as he was himself, but Richard never gave that impression either to me or my son, Simon, who is worthy and an excellent husband, but, to be frank, rather dull. The grandchildren are a delight and Richard was a great success with them and Sophie, his wife, who is a live wire herself, was very fond of him herself. As for Alison, there is no point in beating about the bush. Richard made no secret of the fact that he couldn't get on with her remoteness and seeming lack of interest in the family.'

'I have no wish to embarrass you,' Tyrrell said, 'but from what I've heard so far about your husband, it's obvious that he was a man with a very high libido, in every sense of that word. We already know how driven he was as far as his work was concerned, but inevitably we have also wondered whether he might have been equally so in his personal life, which might have led to serious trouble.'

Lady Elizabeth gave a wintry smile. 'Very tactfully put. You're suggesting that he might have been carrying on an affair with a married woman and that a jealous husband, or partner, which appears to be the current euphemism, might have decided to do something about it.'

'Exactly.'

'I liked and respected Richard enormously. He more than kept his side of the bargain we made and, in return, I turned a blind eye to his extramarital activities. Occasionally, I supported him at his work, for example, those occasions, such as the visit of the late Queen Mother to the hospital, when it would have been both discourteous and insulting to him not to have attended.

'It follows from what I have just said that I knew nothing at all about his private life away from home. The one person whom I would trust to be straightforward and discreet, should you wish to follow up that line, is my brother, James. He knew Richard for many more years than I did and although he likes to give the impression of being a fop and a dunderhead, he is neither.'

'What about the rest of the Brantley family?'

'I haven't seen either my mother or my elder brother, Rupert, since we moved to Highgate. I strongly suspect that he would have liked to stop Richard's allowance long before the agreement ran out, but my father probably had the same concern about it because he had made the arrangement watertight.'

'And Parker?'

'You must already have sensed how much I appreciate him. He has been a calming influence as far as I am concerned; he has always been there for me, but he has never been intrusive. Had it not been for him, I doubt if I would have been able to get through the whole business as well as I have and it was a great bonus that he and Richard should have liked each other.'

'Well, thank you for being so frank,' Tyrrell said. 'I know how much it must have cost you to go back over the past, but it has been a great help to me for your domestic situation to have been made so much clearer. I'm sure you understand that we will have to do everything possible to discover who was responsible for Richard Kershaw's death, but we will also bear in mind the need to protect you and your children from unnecessary publicity.'

Tyrrell was in a sombre mood when Sarah drove him back to London.

'Thanks for your help,' he said.

'I didn't do anything, sir.'

'Oh, but you did. I have an instinct that Lady Elizabeh would not have opened up so much had I been alone with her.'

'But what a really tragic and terrible story.'

'Yes, and she was right. Publicity about her rape and the events that surrounded her marriage and the birth of the twins would undoubtedly have seriously damaged her life and that of several other people as well. Needless to say, for the time being, the information we have obtained from her must remain confidential and I'm sure you'll convey that to Mark.'

Eric Tredgold, the forensic pathologist, was for once in

the best of form, giving the three detectives a beaming smile when they were shown into his office.

'Good to see that the distinguished triumvirate are operating together again,' he said. 'It's been far too long since I saw you all and I have been suffering from withdrawal symptoms. It can hardly be a coincidence, either, that for once Miss Graves should have a smile on her face. What is it that's freed you from the daily grind of administration, my dear Tyrrell? Put your foot in it for once, have you, my dear fellow?'

'You are not the only one to have come to that conclusion, Eric, but no, it seems that the powers that be thought that the toffs brigade, as we have been labelled in the past, was required when the distinguished neurosurgeon, Richard Kershaw, married to Lady Elizabeth, one of the Brantley family, was murdered.'

'Ah, yes. That would explain it and I should have made the connection – must be losing my grip. It might also explain why the victim appears to have enjoyed a sexual variation, which is alleged to be favoured by those "wot speak proper".'

'So, he went in for a touch of flagellation, did he?' Tyrrell said.

Tredgold let out a loud guffaw. 'Is there no end to the man's perspicacity? More than a touch, in fact. The bruising on the man's buttocks was quite irregular, with some of the strokes inflicted crossing each other, as indeed was the force with which they were applied. All that might suggest an amateur, rather than a professional who specializes in that sort of thing, might have been responsible for inflicting it.'

Tredgold operated the keys on his computer and then turned it round so that the three detectives had a good view, then looked across at Sarah Prescott, raising his eyebrows slightly.

'Any comments, young lady? I seem to remember that at one time you worked on the lowlife in Soho.'

Sarah was on home ground and for once didn't give the forensic pathologist the satisfaction of seeing her blush.

'Yes, I agree that the irregular pattern and force of the blows suggest that it was carried out by an amateur, as you said, probably a female one. So far, we have had no hint that Kershaw was a homosexual. The instrument was probably a thin cane. Having said that, flagellation of that sort is a money spinner and prostitutes specializing in that type of thing are not difficult to find, if one knows where to look, particularly in big cities. It is very rare indeed for one of them to agree to have it inflicted on themselves with any force; some of them will allow a gentle spanking, or even a light application of the cane, but most of them fight shy of that altogether. As for amateurs, curiously women are more likely to agree to having it inflicted on them, rather than dishing it out themselves. The psychologists have had a field day trying to explain why that should be.'

Tredgold raised his eyebrows. 'What erudition, to be sure! You have met the man's wife, Tyrrell. Do you think she might have been responsible?'

'I think that highly unlikely,' the detective said. 'Lady Elizabeth is a fastidious, precise and very controlled woman and I don't see her being prepared to do anything of that sort. As for Kershaw, he was, by all accounts, a very driven man and it seems likely that he had a high libido and, in my view, was just the type to have taken advantage of any sexual opportunities outside marriage, amateur or professional.'

Tredgold nodded. 'As to the cause of death, that is straight forward enough. It was due to a severe head injury to the posterior part of the skull delivered by the piece of tubular scaffolding that the industrious Pocock found resting against the wall of the garage. Curious that – in my experience, murderers who use such violent methods, if the deed is premeditated, usually dispose of the weapon in some way or other. If it is done on the spur of the moment, it is usually abandoned at the site, but not left tidily against a wall. There are no rules in his business, though, and I wouldn't put to much emphasis on that.'

'I don't suppose there were any useful fingerprints or DNA found on the murder weapon.' Tyrrell said. 'No doubt you have already found those of the gardener, who some weeks earlier brought it in from the garden after he had found it lying in the undergrowth and then set it against the wall in the garage. Specimens from both him and the manservant who found the body should be with you very soon.'

'Yes, they have been delivered, but testing is still in train and hasn't been completed yet.'

'Would a woman have been able to apply the degree of force that was used on Kershaw?' Tyrrell asked.

'Most certainly and she wouldn't have had to be an Amazon, either.'

CHAPTER FIVE

Back at the Yard, Tyrrell brought Sinclair up to speed with what he and Sarah had learned about the tragic events they had uncovered during his interview with Lady Elizabeth.

'I'm tied up for the rest of the day, so Mark, would you see what Pocock has got for us in that flat, and Sarah, I'd like you to have a go at finding out what you can about the man who raped Lady Elizabeth and then committed suicide. We know the precise date on which it occurred, as it was the night of her coming-of-age ball, and we also know that he was an in-patient at one of the Surrey mental hospitals at that time. It should be easy enough to track down his past history, but it is very much in Lady Elizabeth's interests that neither the press, or indeed anyone else for the time being, get the faintest sniff of your enquiries. I'll get on to the chief of the regional constabulary right away and see if I can fix an appointment up for you with the local records' officer.'

It proved no problem and Sarah met the man a couple of hours later. He turned out to be a cheerful, rotund man in his middle fifties and had taken on the job following his retirement as a sergeant in the uniform branch of the local force. He greeted her with a warm smile, introduced himself as Bert Warren and took her into his office.

'Care for a coffee, ma'am?' he said.

'I certainly would, the drive down was a nightmare – roadworks on the A3.'

'Hang on a moment then, ma'am, and I'll bring it in here.'

The man came back a short time later with a cafetière and some chocolate biscuits.

'That's wonderful, Bert. How did you achieve that miracle?'

The man gave her a broad grin. 'I have a small cubbyhole through there. It's got an electric point in it, with a small fridge and the kettle which I brought here when I started the job. My Ethel deals with the provisions and I'm able to outdo the canteen; not difficult as they only serve up instant and stale rich tea biscuits.'

Sarah gave him a smile. 'My boss uses the same trick and it's a life saver.'

'No need to hurry with your drink, ma'am. It may take me a bit of time to find what you're looking for. There are one or two magazines over there, which you might like to look at.'

To Sarah's surprise, the man reappeared only some twenty minutes later.

'Not a very testing assignment, ma'am,' he said with a broad smile, 'even though the events in question occurred a long time ago. It's not often that I'm given an exact date with an incident occurring more than twenty-five years ago, or that I'm given so much information about it, even a comment about the weather. It seems that the weekend of the 10/11 July 1982 was warm and humid and indeed violent thunderstorms occurred in the South-west of the country at that time. However, the rain didn't come to these parts until later, because if it had, the man might well not have been found so quickly.

'You see, it was early in the morning of Sunday 11 July of that year that the dead man was found by a middle-aged woman walking her dog in the woods, not all that far from here.' Warren unfolded the Ordnance Survey map and pointed to the small cross which had been pencilled in. 'That's the spot.' He gave a chuckle. 'They're pretty tough those no-nonsense, Labrador owning, stout-booted and tweed-skirted women around here. It was, of course, before the days of mobile phones and as she lived not far away, she strode back to her place, telephoned us and then went back to the site to warn off any other walkers who might have come across the man. You can see from this photo that he was not a pretty sight. He had obviously climbed up the tree, then hanged himself with the belt from his trousers.

'There was no problem in identifying him. His name was Alan Crosby and he had been reported missing a couple of days earlier from St Olave's, a mental hospital about ten miles from the place where he was found. One of the doctors there gave us his name and some details about him. Evidently, the fellow was a paranoid schizophrenic. There are several photographs of him here taken during his time in the hospital and also of the scene of his suicide. You'll also find the report of the inquest, which includes evidence from the psychiatrist who was in charge of his case and the forensic pathologist. I'll leave you in peace to read it through, but give us a shout of you have any queries.'

'Thank you very much. You've been most helpful'

After looking at the photographs, Sarah read through the papers carefully, starting with the pathologist's report. His estimate of the time of death was between 11 p.m. and 2 a.m. on the night of 10/11 July 1982. The man was wearing town shoes, shirt, sweater, under-pants and trousers and probably had not shaved for at least forty-eight hours. He was well nourished, but mildly dehydrated. He had ejaculated a short time before his death and, there had been no report of any rapes that night in the area, it seemed most likely that the hanging was the reason, an occurrence which was well recorded. There were a few coins in one pocket and a dirty handkerchief in the other, plus a scrumpled up page, which had been torn out of a magazine.

Details of the next of kin, his mother, Helen Crosby, had been obtained from the hospital notes and in her evidence at the inquest she stated that on the last occasion that she had visited her son a few days before his death, he had seemed agitated, but wouldn't tell her what was wrong. She was sufficiently concerned about him to have reported it to the staff nurse on duty. She was told that there was nothing to worry about as, although family and visitors were always welcome, some patients found those visits stressful and unsettling and that that was the probable explanation for his upset.

Sarah was sitting at the desk, deep in thought, when Bert Warren returned.

'Got everything you wanted, ma'am?'

'Pretty well, thank you, Bert, but it would be extremely helpful if you would photocopy the pages I have set aside plus the photograph of the man in the wood and the magazine cutting.'

'I'll do my best, ma'am, but I doubt if they'll come out all that clear.'

As the man had warned her, the results weren't exactly impressive, but good enough for her immediate requirements.

'Thank you so much. My superior can always come down here to look at the originals for himself, but I doubt if that will be necessary. And Bert!'

'Yes, ma'am.'

'This enquiry is extremely tricky and I'd be most grateful if you would keep quiet about my visit here and not mention it to anyone at all. I'm afraid that I can't tell you the reason why but I assure you that that's very important.'

'All you've found out is extremely interesting,' Tyrrell said when Sarah reported to him, 'particularly that cutting. You did well to get it dated and it is obviously highly significant that it was an announcement of the ball for Lady Elizabeth Brantley's eighteenth birthday, which was to be held on the same evening that the man committed suicide.'

'Yes, and it seems more than likely that the same man was the rapist, although at the time it would have been impossible to prove because the ability to detect

DNA from semen wasn't achieved until 1985 and was used for the first time in the Pitchfork murder case a year later. In any case, Lady Elizabeth wasn't examined from a forensic point of view after the incident so that even the man's blood grouping wouldn't have been discovered.'

'What about his mother, Helen Crosby? I imagine it's too much to hope that she's still alive.'

'Well, sir, it appears that she is. I got Fred in records to look her up in the 2001 census and she was certainly alive then at the same address as we have for Crosby in the police file.'

'And that was?'

'Fairmile Cottage, which is in a village only a few miles from the hospital where her son, Alan, was an in-patient. Luckily the place still has a post office, which is in the village shop. I gave it a ring and the postmistress told me that Mrs Crosby was still there, a bit frail physically, but still quite sharp mentally. I thought it best to ask the woman not to mention our interest in her to anyone, particularly Mrs Crosby herself, as we were proposing to visit her and had no wish to worry her in advance.'

'Excellent work, Sarah, and also very interesting. I think we should go to see her as soon as possible, perhaps tomorrow morning. That would give me an excuse to get out of a tedious meeting. How about Mark? How is he getting on?'

'He wouldn't give me any details as he hadn't finished yet in the flat, but he did say that Pocock had shown him some very interesting stuff there, which he was going to collate with a view to showing us very soon.'

Tyrrell nodded. 'I'm looking forward to seeing what he has uncovered.'

At first, there was no audible response to Tyrrell's knock on the door of Fairmile Cottage, then they heard footsteps and the door was opened on its chain.

'Yes, who is it?'

The voice was soft, but there was no hint of a quaver in it.

'Mrs Crosby?' Tyrrell said, showing the woman both their warrant cards. 'Chief Superintendent Tyrrell and Detective Inspector Prescott. We're making enquiries about an incident that occurred a long time ago, getting on for thirty years, in fact, and we believe that your son's death may have had something to do with it.'

There was a long silence and then the chain was disengaged.

'I was very pleased to see you using the chain,' Tyrrell said with a smile, when they were standing in the small entrance hall. 'I wish everyone was that sensible.'

The elderly woman inclined her head slightly. 'It's not often that I have visitors and if what I read about the police visiting, in the detective stories I like to read, is true, then perhaps tea or coffee is just what is required.'

'Coffee would be more than welcome,' Tyrrell said. 'Would you like my assistant to help you?'

'That would be most kind,' she said, smiling at Sarah. 'I'm sure your time is precious and I'm pretty slow at doing anything these days.'

Tyrrell waited in the easy chair in the sitting room and then got to his feet as the old lady came back through the door ten minutes later, followed by Sarah, who was carrying a tray on which was a coffee pot, a jug of cream, sugar bowl and a plate of biscuits as well as three cups and saucers.

'They take their time, these filter machines,' Mrs Crosby said, when, under her instructions, Sarah poured out the drinks, 'but I, for one, think it's worth the wait.'

'I couldn't agree more,' Tyrrell said, after taking a sip, 'delicious!'

'Yes, it's Colombian and Mrs Porter at the post office always make sure that there is some available for me. It's one of my weaknesses.'

Tyrrell nodded. 'My favourite, too. Now, I assure you that it was with considerable reluctance that we felt it necessary to invade your privacy. You may have seen or heard that a distinguished London surgeon was murdered on the Sunday before last. His wife is a member of the Brantley family, who still live on the estate not all that far from here.'

The old lady stared at him for a few moments and then said: 'And even closer to where my son committed suicide.'

'Yes and that made us wonder why he should have been there, particularly as a cutting from a magazine was found in one of his pockets announcing that a ball was to be held there by the late Lord Brantley to mark the eighteenth birthday of his daughter, Lady Elizabeth. The same Lady Elizabeth was the wife of the surgeon, Richard Kershaw, the man who was killed.'

There was a very long pause and then the old lady slowly nodded her head.

'I've been wanting to get this off my chest for well in

excess of sixty years and now is as good a time as any. It was in July 1944 a few weeks after D-Day and I was a nineteen year old ATS driver, having taken a motor-transport course earlier that summer in England. I was stationed in Northern France and worked as the driver of the adjutant of an infantry regiment, one Captain the Honourable William Brantley. One of his duties was to visit casualties in the field hospital in Bayeux, where a number of them were still too ill to be transported back home.

'One of the most painful tasks he had to tackle was writing to the next of kin of those who had died. I'll say this for William, he never just sent out formula letters. If he had known the man personally, he would find out something about him that would make it clear that he had genuinely cared for him and pointed out what a sad loss it had been for all his many friends. If he hadn't known the man, he would take the trouble to find out something creditable or touching about his character and put it into an appropriate form.

'Driving around at that time was fraught with both danger and frustration. There were enormous pot- and shell-holes in the roads, tanks were constantly rumbling past us and we were occasionally strafed from the air. I got carried along by the excitement of it all and to some extent by the pride I felt about being so personally involved.

'The day it happened was a particularly fraught one. Messages had been coming in all morning, it was pouring with rain and it took us twice as long as usual to get to the hospital. When we got there, he asked me if I would come with him to see one particular soldier, whom William knew personally, and who was not expected to last more than another twenty-four hours. He had been horribly injured and I sat with him for half an hour while William did his round and tried to talk to him about anything other than the war and his injuries. Most of his face was obscured by bandages, but there was still intelligence both in his one visible eye and the little squeezes he gave me as I talked to him and I like to think that it helped.

'William hardly spoke a word to me on the way back, but when we arrived at the base, he said: "It was very brave of you to sit with that young fellow and I know how much your presence meant to him and what a comfort it was. He told me so just before we left."

'It was a heart-rending time for both of us and at the end of that awful day, he got hold of a bottle of wine and yes, I finished up in his room. A lot of girls of my age with respectable working-class backgrounds were pretty naïve in those days and I was more so than most. It began with a comforting hug when I broke down under the influence of the unaccustomed alcohol and we ended up in bed together. I got pregnant and that was that.

'To William's credit, he didn't just abandon me and, according to his lights, he didn't behave badly at all. He explained about his Catholicism and Opus Dei, with which you are no doubt familiar, although it wasn't until much later that I found out exactly what that involved. Anyway, a termination was out of the question and William made it quite clear that he wouldn't be able to keep in touch with me or the child personally. Both my parents had been killed in London in the Blitz while I had been evacuated to a family in Wales, who, even though they hadn't treated me badly, clearly resented my presence and were only too glad to see the back of me when I joined up at the age of eighteen in early 1944.

'As a result, I had no one to turn to and accepted what William had arranged for me through his solicitor. He bought the freehold of this cottage for me with no strings attached and I was given a modest allowance for life. Money wasn't and hasn't been a problem. I was careful with that allowance and the salary from the secretarial job I found later on, and with my old-age pension and the savings I made, I have enough to live comfortably.'

'And when was it that your son was taken ill?'

'As a young boy, Alan was no trouble at all. He was very quiet and never found it easy to make friends, but when he was sixteen he got a job as an apprentice in a local factory, which made parts for domestic appliances and it was a couple of years later that the problems started. It began with his complaining that the others were talking about him and soon after he began to hear voices. Within a matter of weeks, he lost his job and the last straw came when he attacked me here, hitting me on the head with a metal saucepan and shouting out that I had been putting poison in his food.'

'And was it following that distressing incident that he was admitted to the mental hospital?'

'Yes. The psychiatrist told me that Alan was suffering from paranoid schizophrenia and that I was in real danger from him. The man was very kind and reassured me that the condition was a chemical abnormality in the brain and that in no way was I to blame for what had happened. I have to admit at first I thought he was just trying to reassure me, but then I did some reading about it and that was what finally took some of the load off my shoulders.'

'Was your son able to come home at any stage?'

'Not for any length of time. The really sad thing was that during the few weeks before he died, Alan was showing signs of real improvement and was even able to spend a couple of weekends with me here, the last time being about ten days before he ran away from the hospital.'

'Did you at any time tell him about his father and what happened after his birth?'

'Yes, I did, when he was eighteen, before his illness had become apparent. Of course, I have regretted it ever since he started to get symptoms a few years later, even though the psychiatrist told me that I had done the right thing and that it had nothing to do with his schizophrenia. "I can assure you," he said, "that in my experience it is far better to adopt the way you chose, rather than for the person to discover circumstances like that by chance later on".'

'I wanted to believe him, but once Alan became progressively more deluded and was hearing disturbing voices, it never left my mind, and his suicide so close to his father's estate brought all my concerns back. You mentioned earlier the cutting that was found on Alan; I take that magazine and when the police asked me about it, I checked my copy and realized that Alan must have torn it out when he came to stay for the weekend about two weeks earlier, something I hadn't noticed before.'

'Did your son mention having seen the announcement about the ball to you?'

'No, he didn't, but I can't help thinking that with the improvement in his mental state, it must have been the last straw to have discovered about his half-sister like that. It's true that in the past, at the worst time of his illness, he had talked about that whole family as having been spawned by the devil and perhaps seeing the announcement and watching the guests arriving for that ball and the luxury, which was in such stark contrast to his own situation, may have been what tipped him over.'

'Did you see your son after he had taken the cutting?'

'No. At that time I was having a serious flare-up of my rheumatoid arthritis and I really ought to have been in hospital. By that time, too, there was a different psychiatrist in charge of Alan's case and he told me that my son had been very upset by the deterioration in my health and recommended that I should get over the worst of the relapse before seeing him again. That made good sense to me at the time and it still does. Would it have made any difference if I had noticed that Alan had torn out that piece about Elizabeth Brantley? I like to think not.'

'I'm quite sure you're right about that,' Tyrrell said. 'In your situation, I would have been pleased that Alan was showing an interest in the family and that it was wholly understandable that he wouldn't have wanted to share the burden with you when you were so obviously unwell.'

'Do you really believe that?'

'I most certainly do.'

The old lady nodded. 'I must say that that gives me at least some comfort. You know, I never bore William any ill will. I was as much to blame for what happened as he was, even taking into account the difference in our ages, and the settlement he made for me was a generous one. Did he know about Alan's suicide? I like to believe that he didn't. After all, it wasn't reported in the national press and he must have been ill at the time himself, as he died not long after.'

'I'm sure you're right.'

'Do you think so?'

Tyrrell looked straight at her. 'Yes, I do. You see, I have discovered that Lord Brantley had been suffering from heart trouble in the several weeks leading up to the ball and was only well enough to put in a short token appearance at the event. What happened to your allowance after his death?'

'It was stopped, but by then I had enough put by to manage comfortably on my own. The solicitor, who was dealing with it, took the trouble to contact me and explained what had happened. Evidently, after William had his first heart attack, he went to see him and once he had discovered that I had been careful with the money and would be financially secure if the allowance was stopped, the arrangement was wound up. The remaining capital was donated to the National Heart Foundation anonymously and on the condition that there was no publicity. The solicitor was obviously relieved that I was satisfied by the way the whole thing had been handled. I have no reason to suppose that anyone in William's other family know anything about the arrangement that had been made for me, or indeed about my association with him, and that is the way I would like it to remain.'

'I fully understand that,' Tyrrell said, 'and I don't believe that there is any reason why they should ever find out.'

'What a sad story,' Sarah said, as she drove Tyrrell back to London.

'Yes. At least the poor woman doesn't appear to have any idea that her son raped Lady Elizabeth. Also, from what James Brantley told me, there is a good chance that Lord Brantley was not Lady Elizabeth's father and if that is true, she was not a blood relative of Alan Crosby. What we've heard also makes one understand why Lord Brantley pulled out all the stops to prevent the press getting hold of the sad story of the rape, particularly if he thought they were half-brother and sister.

'I don't see how this whole wretched business could conceivably have had anything to do with Richard Kershaw's murder,' Tyrrell continued. 'It's only fair that you should tell Mark about it, but apart from him, I don't want anyone else, and I mean anyone, to know about what that poor woman has just told us. Are you happy to go along with that?'

Sarah didn't hesitate. 'It's nearly thirty years since Lady Elizabeth was raped and, as you said, there seems no way that that could be tied up with Kershaw's murder. Just imagine, too, what publicity and the knowledge that her son was a rapist and that twin children had resulted from it, would do to Mrs Crosby. There are also Lady Elizabeth and her children to think about. I am with you all the way on this, sir, and I know that Mark will be, too. Neither of us will so much as hint that we've even seen the old lady.'

'Good,' said Tyrrell. 'I knew I could rely on you both and I take full responsibility for the decision.'

Pocock was sitting in the corner of Miss Perry's office studying a typewritten list with intense concentration when the doorbell sounded.

'That will be Inspector Sinclair,' he said, glancing at his watch and giving the woman the hint of a smile. 'A very punctual gentleman, he is. Don't let us disturb you, though, Miss Perry. I'll let him in and we'll let you know when we have finished in the other rooms.'

'What treasures have you uncovered, Jack?' Sinclair asked, after Pocock had introduced him to the secretary and they were standing in the corridor.

'I'd best show you, sir, but first I'd like to give a small demonstration. If you'd care to wait here, I'll only be a moment.'

'Sounds intriguing.'

The detective watched as Pocock manipulated the numbers on the entry pad on the wall by the entrance to the master bedroom, opened the door just wide enough to let himself in and then shut it behind himself.

'What on earth is the man up to?' Sinclair said to himself after he had been standing there for several minutes, the only sounds being those coming from the traffic in the square outside.

'Right, sir, I'm ready now,' Pocock said when the door swung open.

The room was quite a bit larger than the one that was used as Miss Perry's office and contained a king-sized double bed, a built-in wardrobe along one side and a second door, which led to the bathroom, which was also substantial, with a bath, shower, lavatory and a large cupboard, which contained an unvented, high-pressure hot water system.

'Does away with the need for a water tank, sir, and also takes care of both the central heating system and the hot water.'

'Yes,' Sinclair said, 'they're very efficient. My brother has one and swears by it.'

Pocock nodded. 'Now, sir, I'd like to carry out a small experiment.'

The man burrowed into his bag, pulled out a large balloon and inflated it from a small cylinder before tying it off. What on earth is the man playing at, the detective wondered, as Pocock held it at arm's length and then plunged the sharp tip of the spike on his penknife into it, the balloon exploding with a loud bang.

'Steady on, Jack, you'll frighten the horses.'

The man's lugubrious expression didn't alter as he delved into the bag again and pulled out the remains of a second shattered balloon.

'I carried out the same experiment with this one while you were waiting outside the door, sir. Did you hear anything?'

Sinclair shook his head. 'Not a sound and now you mention it, there is no suspicion of traffic noise in here, which was very obvious out in the corridor.'

'That's because this room and the bathroom have been most efficiently soundproofed. The walls, the floors

113

and the ceilings have all been dealt with compre-
hensively.'

'Must have cost a bomb and, off the top of my head, I
can only think of one reason for Kershaw having done
it and that is that he might have liked entertaining the
ladies in here.'

Any normal man, Sinclair thought, would have
expressed surprise, disappointment or even both at his
having hit the nail on the head, but from long
experience, he knew that Pocock didn't do surprise: he
had seen it all before.

'Yes, indeed, sir. As to the cost, we found the
paperwork in that chest of drawers over there. It
appears that he paid for all the work here in cash and I
rather doubt if it went through the books of the firms
that did it. There are receipts here, but none of them is
on headed paper and the signatures are illegible.'

'Bit of a risk, that, I would have thought,' Sinclair
said, 'but presumably he didn't want to run any danger
of the contractors being traced. Perhaps, too, as judged
by his skill at wood carving and furniture, Kershaw
knew enough to supervise the work himself and test the
soundproofing. Presumably you've done that yourself
with a meter.'

'Yes, sir. We've checked various sites both inside the
other rooms in the flat and also in the corridors and in
the flats above and below and also outside in the street.'

'And nothing significant carried?'

'Nothing. We generated considerable noise levels both
in the room and the bathroom and the results were
negative.'

'I wonder what the neighbours thought of all the

work that Kershaw arranged to be done, and indeed your own enquiries?'

'That is not recorded, sir, and I thought it best not to try to find out at this stage. I did discover, though, that it was all carried out before Miss Perry was employed here.'

'And presumably the object of the exercise was to allow fun and games to occur without disturbing the natives.'

'Yes, one might be justified in making that assumption, sir.'

Sinclair was hard pressed not to react to the man's extraordinarily stilted way of putting things, even though he was all too familiar with it.

'Then I take it that there is plenty of evidence to that contention?'

My God, thought Sinclair, the man's stilted way of speaking is contagious. To his relief, Pocock didn't react to his remark verbally, although his body language strongly suggested that he would have liked to have done so.

'As you see, sir, there is a flat TV screen over there with connections to a DVD player and a tape recorder and in those cupboards behind us is a tripod and still and television cameras.'

'And no doubt sex toys as well.'

'Yes, sir, including a variety of restraints, vibrators and instruments of correction.'

'And in view of the post-mortem evidence, the last named were mainly for use by female on male?'

If Pocock was surprised by Sinclair's remark, he didn't show it.

'As judged by the films I have viewed, that was the case except for the occasional use of very thin straps on a few of the women, which would not, in my opinion, have left visible marks of any duration.'

'Many different women involved?'

'Not recently, sir. The various episodes have been dated and within in the last nine months or so they have all involved the same young woman, but before that there was quite a variety of them.'

'What would you say were the chances of identifying the most recent one?'

Pocock turned towards the line of built-in, full-length cupboards behind them.

'Perhaps you'd care to look at some of the most recent pictures, sir, which explain the problem? I haven't, though, had time to study them all in detail.'

'Thank you, Jack. Carry on.'

The images, both still and moving were in sharp focus and were of excellent quality.

'Perhaps when you've had a chance to view them all, Jack, you would make a selection so that Mr Tyrrell and Inspector Prescott will be able to view the significant ones without having to spend too much time on them. A few of those from the past would also be useful, but I would like you to concentrate on those taken within the last nine months and I am particularly interested in any identifiable marks on the body of that particular young woman and any rings she might have been wearing.'

'Very good, sir. I'll see to it this afternoon.'

'What about costumes, Jack?'

'On the evidence of those I have viewed briefly, the

women weren't wearing them all that often, but there is a selection in those two wardrobes over there and some interesting photographic stills as well as some commercially produced pornography.' The man turned toward the detective. 'I have catalogued them, sir, according to the particular subject matter, which I hope will make your task of looking through them easier.'

Sinclair looked for any sign of disapproval or amusement on the man's face, but, as he expected, there wasn't the merest hint of a change from his normal lugubrious expression.

'Thank you, Jack, but before you go, I'd like you to show me what you can about how and when Kershaw came by those marks on his backside.'

'I thought that might be the case, sir, and I've already set up the bedclothes as they were when the pictures were taken.'

Pocock opened up one of the cupboards, took out a tripod and set up the video camera on it. 'If you care to look through the view finder, sir, you will see that the whole of the double bed is in view and with one simple adjustment it can be made to focus on the centre.'

Sinclair had already observed that the bed was covered by a single sheet and that there were two pillows, one at the head and the other in the centre.

'Now, sir, you were asking about the marks on the man's buttocks. It appears that the beatings were carried out on a fairly regular basis ever since the recordings with this particular woman were started and if you care to sit facing the screen, I will find the relevant clips for you. There is a selection of canes, paddles and riding crops in that wardrobe over there and I'll get the instrument that was used most frequently for you.'

The cane had a crook handle and Sinclair swished it through the air a few times.

'Not a particularly fearsome weapon,' Sinclair said, 'but no doubt heavy enough to produce the marks on the man's body.'

The video clearly showed Kershaw, ankles and wrists cuffed, shuffling naked across the carpet. Once he was lying face down on the bed, first his ankles were released, his legs spread wide and then first one and then the other was attached to the bottom legs of the bed by chains. The manoeuvre was then repeated, this time with the wrists being secured at the other end.

The woman, who was also naked apart from an elaborate headdress, which completely covered her face and hair, apart from slits for her eyes, whispered something in the man's ear. She then picked up the cane and brought it whistling down, each blow followed by a convulsive jerk from the spread-eagled man.

'Right, thank you, Jack. I've seen enough to get the general idea and it certainly explains how Kershaw came by those marks and exactly when. He was murdered on Sunday ten days ago and you say that this video was taken on the preceding Thursday.'

'That is correct, sir. The machine was left recording for some thirty-five minutes from about 11 p.m. that evening.'

'From what I could see in that admittedly short clip, there were no obvious marks on the young woman's skin that might help us to identify her, but perhaps you would get the experts to look carefully for any evidence of that in any of the other takes that featured her.'

'Very good, sir. In the ones I have scanned briefly, her head and hair have invariably been covered by a variety of masks and headdresses, all of which are in that wardrobe over there and we should be able to get her DNA from a number of them. It is almost certain that she is the only woman to have been featured in the clips taken within the last nine months or so and we should be able to prove that in due course.'

'What about the other women featured earlier on? Were they identifiable?'

'No, sir. In every case, care had been taken to obscure their faces.'

'Were any of them subjected to sadistic sex play?'

'No, sir, apart from being loosely tied up on occasions and fairly gently spanked. From all the ones I have glanced at, the man certainly seems to have enjoyed being humiliated himself in all sorts of ways and there was never any force applied to the women, who almost always took the dominant role.'

'Did he have full sex with all of them?'

'We will be able to provide all the details in due course, sir, but the selection I viewed at random would suggest that conclusion.'

'You've already told me that there were no identifiable marks on the body of Kershaw's latest lady friend, but what about her voice?'

'The recordings are unlikely to be rewarding, I would say, sir. I'll show you what I mean by playing an example of her speaking and you'll see what I mean.'

Pocock slotted in another cassette and pressed a button on the handset of the video recorder and an image of the naked man, with wrists and ankles attached by straps to the corners of the bed, sprang into view.

'I've warned you before about your behaviour, you snivelling cur, and now comes the time of reckoning.'

Pocock switched off the machine and turned towards the detective. 'No expense spared. Two cameras were used, one focused on the man on the bed and the other on the woman, with voice recorders for both and some clever editing done later. Any views on the woman's voice, sir?'

'At first, I was wondering if she was using one of those fancy voice-altering machines, but it sounded to me as if she had something in her mouth – a plum, perhaps?'

Not so much as a flicker of amusement crossed Pocock's face. It was almost, Sinclair thought, as if the lugubrious man hadn't understood his admittedly feeble joke.

'Yes, sir. That was the conclusion I also arrived at, too. She spoke in the same way on all the tapes in which she appeared.'

'Was that true of the other women?'

'No sir, they all used normal voices.'

'Interesting! With that and the headdresses it seems more than likely that Kershaw was taking special care to hide the identity of his most recent partner in the unlikely event of anyone getting hold of the tapes. Was that particular woman ever on the receiving end of the various instruments of punishment?'

'He did spank her a few times, but not all that hard and on the occasions that he tied her up, she made no attempt to free herself, although she could easily have done so.'

'What else did he do to her on those occasions?'

'I'll show you, if you like, sir.'

When he saw the clip, Sinclair was not in the least surprised that Pocock had preferred not to give him an oral summary. The young woman had been tied up and Kershaw had gone to work on her body with a feather, making intimate contacts with her until she completely lost control, moaning and crying out and finally begging him to desist.

Sinclair raised his eyebrows when Pocock switched off the machine. 'And not a sound would have been heard outside, even after that bravura performance, Jack?'

'No, sir. You already know about the exploding balloons, sir, but we also played loud music, shouted and hit the pillow as hard as we could with one of the canes and absolutely nothing could be heard in the rest of the flat, in those adjacent on each side, above, below or on the pavement outside.'

CHAPTER SIX

The two detectives met Tyrrell in his office the following morning at 8.30.

'As you know,' he said, 'we've arranged to see Jack at Kershaw's flat at nine, but first of all, Mark, I wanted to bring you up to date with what Sarah and I discovered yesterday. It's not that I don't trust you Mark, but, as I hope it will become clear, I don't want to risk letting what we heard from Lady Elizabeth and the information we obtained from one Mrs Crosby getting into the public domain. That would most certainly blight a great many lives.'

Before going into that, Tyrrell gave a succinct account of his talks with Lady Elizabeth, her daughter and brother.

'And so you see, if ever there was a tangled web, this is certainly it. Lady Elizabeth is almost certainly the illegitimate daughter of the dowager Marchioness and her own twins are the consequence of her rape by the schizophrenic son of Mrs Crosby, who himself was the result of his mother's liaison with the late Marquis during the war.' He raised his eyebrows. 'I hope that

makes at least some sense to you. Both the late
Marquis and his successor, his legitimate elder son,
were and are members of Opus Dei and therefore
termination of either pregnancy was never an option.

'In order to tidy things up, Richard Kershaw agreed
to marry Lady Elizabeth, but only in name, and part of
the deal was for him to stay with her in the house in
Highgate, which was bequeathed to her. It is also clear
that they made a joint decision about the way they were
going to conduct their marriage. They decided that they
would reside in the same house, but the rest of their
lives, particularly the sex side of it, would be entirely
independent.' He paused and then looked across at
Sinclair, then gave him an account of Sarah's visit to
the police station and their later interview with Mrs
Crosby. 'I hope that is all reasonably clear, Mark.'

Sinclair raised his eyebrows slightly, then nodded. 'I
think so, sir.'

'Right. What did you and Jack manage to dig up in
that flat?'

'I think it would be best if I were to show you on site,
sir.'

Tyrrell glanced at his watch. 'Very well, we'd better
get there right away.'

As soon as they arrived at the flat and Sinclair had
introduced Miss Perry to Tyrrell and Sarah, Pocock
showed them the layout of the flat and demonstrated
the soundproofing in the en suite bedroom and
bathroom in much the same way as he had done with
Sinclair and then played them a selection of the earlier
tapes.

'Any comments about all that, Sarah?' Tyrrell asked. 'You worked on the vice squad for quite some time and know about these things.'

'Yes, sir. All the women we have seen so far were almost certainly all prostitutes. Clearly, quite a few of them were foreigners and, despite the variety of sexual acts that went on, kissing was notable for its absence. That is something that very few women on the game will agree to do.'

'Thank you,' said Tyrrell. 'Perhaps you'd carry on, Jack.'

Without delay, the man restarted the video recorder and at the end of that series of clips Sarah was asked for her further comments.

'As is quite clear, the whole attitude and behaviour of the last of the women is strikingly different from all the others. Not only does she appear invariably to have worn a variety of headdresses, all of which completely obscured her hair and face, except her mouth, but sessions with her were much longer and more elaborate and there is no doubt that she was a much more enthusiastic participant than any of the others, both when applying the instruments of correction to Kershaw and when taking part in more conventional sexual activity herself. She also happily accepted the type of behaviour which most prostitutes won't countenance, such as anal and oral sex without a condom and she also joined in enthusiastically with every variety of kissing.

'As far as the masks are concerned, it seems to me likely that they were used to make her very difficult to identify, raising the possibility that she had a lot to lose if she had been found out. Her voice was also altered, probably by holding something in her mouth while speaking.'

Tyrrell nodded. 'Thank you, Sarah. That all makes good sense. Any comments, Mark?'

'The fact that both of them made such efforts to hide her identity suggests to me that she is either a family acquaintance, or someone connected with the hospital, probably the latter. It is certainly disappointing, that even with all their tricks of the trade, the experts haven't managed to find any distinguishing marks on her body.'

'Anything to add to all that, Jack?'

'Not much, sir. The photographic people seemed to believe that the only way to identify any suspect from this material would be to photograph the woman using the same headdress and poses and compare the two.'

'That's an unlikely scenario, I must say,' Tyrrell remarked. 'We could hardly expect any female suspect to strip off completely for them. Anyway, the whole set-up and the elaborate steps that Kershaw and the young woman took to prevent her identification all point to her having been well known in either his domestic or hospital life and quite possibly both. However, that doesn't necessarily mean that his activities here had anything to do with his murder.'

'Where do you think that Lady Elizabeth stands in all this, sir?' Sinclair asked.

'I'm convinced that both she and Kershaw entered into their marriage with the same objectives. On his side, he would make the arrival of the twins acceptable, would help in their upbringing and education, join the family on holidays with them and support some of his wife's charitable activities. On her side, Lady Elizabeth would turn up at some hospital events. As far as sex was concerned, I'm pretty sure that after her rape, Lady Elizabeth wanted nothing more to do with it and it was part of the deal that Kershaw should be able to lead that side of his life independently, provided he was discreet about it. He certainly was that when one considers the trouble he took to make this place soundproof. I think it very likely that they both kept their sides of the bargain and I got the strong impression from Lady Elizabeth that she both liked and respected Kershaw as a person and that they were genuinely fond of each other in a purely platonic sense.

'Both their financial situations would also seem to have been secure from the start. Not only did Lady Elizabeth have money of her own, left to her by an aunt, but, when they married, he was obviously a potential high flier in medicine. True, he was only on a junior doctor's pay when they were first married, but that situation didn't last very long and, in any case, right from the start of the marriage they had enough to live on very comfortably. As to the future, Kershaw had some investments, which he has bequeathed to her and she will also get half his NHS pension as his widow.'

'Yes, sir, I see all that, but it was hardly discreet of Kershaw to have chosen a place so close to the hospital for his extramarital sexual activities and surely all along there must have been a good chance that someone would have noticed the various comings and goings.

'I wouldn't be so sure.' Tyrrell said. 'There are a good many flats in this block, and with Kershaw's habit of recording and dating all the details of the arrivals and departures of all those women, we know that he got away with it for all of fifteen years. There's never been any CCTV around here and there are two entrances to this block, one from the square and the other from the street behind. I suppose we could run the faces of those women through our data base of prostitutes, but I can't see how any of them could have been involved with his death, not least because he stopped seeing them almost a year ago.'

'Any chance of DNA having been left by his most recent partner, Jack?' Sarah asked.

'We've already looked for and found that on the headdress, ma'am, the various items of clothing that haven't been laundered and the various instruments of punishment. There is also the question of fingerprints, but if she's not on either data base, that doesn't take us any further until we have a reasonable suspect, when it would be a different matter.'

'The other thing that struck me, apart from the young woman's enthusiastic cooperation with all the fantasies and sexual variations,' Sarah said, 'is that she is the only one to have invariably taken steps to alter her voice.'

'Good point,' said Sinclair. 'That suggests to me that she is either a family acquaintance, possibly known to Lady Elizabeth, or someone connected to the hospital.'

'What sort of conversations were picked up on those recording devices, Jack?' Tyrrell asked.

'Practically all of them, sir, were connected with the

fantasies that the two of them had been playing out, but there were also very brief snatches of endearment after they had finished, but never once did Kershaw use her name. Unfortunately, too, I have been unable to find any examples at all of the woman's unaltered speech.'

'Giving some support to your theory, Mark,' Tyrrell said. 'What had you in mind to do next?'

'I thought I'd have another word with John Fielding to see if there had been any very difficult cases recently resulting in serious complications, which might have led to a disgruntled relative attacking Kershaw. I also think it would be worth trying to find out a bit more about Kershaw's activities away from the hospital. I'm sure you noticed, sir, that there was an expensive set of Callaway golf clubs and a box of Titleist balls in the cloakroom off the hall in the Highgate house, all of which made me green with envy. I'm sure Parker would know which golf club he belonged to. It also looked to me as if the man had been looking after both the shoes and the equipment – they were immaculate.'

'Good idea. Sarah?'

'I got the strong impression that Rebecca Cochrane was concerned about something in connection with Annette Fielding and I'd like to have another informal chat with both of them.'

That afternoon, Mark Sinclair found John Fielding in the office in Kershaw's flat.

'I've been coping with any queries that Miss Perry feels she can't deal with herself,' the surgeon said. 'As you may imagine, it's no easy task. The bulk of our work consists of undertaking non-urgent elective procedures and I have felt it wise not to carry out any of those myself for the time being. It's not that I don't feel capable of doing so, but there are always hazards in any branch of surgery, not least that on the brain, and in these litigious days, I decided it wasn't worth the risk.

'I also thought that it would be good sense to talk to Dr Maitland, who carries more clout here than any of the other surgeons, about the situation. He agreed with my approach and also thought that it would be best for all the emergencies to be handled by the other consultant neurosurgeons.'

'I see. What do you suppose all this is going to do for your future prospects in neurosurgery?'

'Naturally I am concerned about that and I took the opportunity to discuss it with Maitland as well and he was very helpful. He told me that he, personally, felt that this hospital would be lucky to have me on the staff. However, he also pointed out that the neurosurgical set-up here was not the happiest one and already there had been jockeying for position. We had discussed the possibility of a post outside London earlier and he told me that he would be only too happy to act as one of my referees should I choose to make an application if and when one came up.'

'Do you find the idea attractive?'

'At first, I rather doubted if it would be a good career move for me, but Annette clearly likes the idea, not least because we would be living within easy reach of the Isle of Wight, where her parents live. However, reading between the lines of what Maitland said, my chances here might not be as good as he first thought because of a possible reorganization of neurosurgical services in the near future.'

'Your wife's new job, though, has been a success, has it?'

'It certainly has. Her whole attitude has changed recently and it's almost as if she is a different person. Both of us were inexperienced sexually when we married, and, to be honest, that side of things never worked all that well. Quite out of the blue, though, about six months ago, she told me that she had decided to see a female counsellor and it was quite extraordinary what an effect that had and it made me realize what we had been missing. It has been as if someone had pressed a happiness and energy button inside both of us from that point of view.'

'Have you raised the question of a permanent post for you outside London with your wife?'

'Yes, only the other day after I had had that chat with Maitland.'

'I hope it works out well for you.'

'Thank you, but Kershaw's murder is not going to make it easy for me, whatever Maitland says.'

'In what way?'

'Annette told me that she had heard whisperings that Kershaw's death had not come a moment too soon for me, because, even with him gone, I had been chained to him for so long that I would never be able to function on my own, away from the guidance of the master. If that sort of innuendo is being bandied about and I'm quite sure that it is – Annette would never make up anything like that – then it's not exactly going to help me find powerful backers and referees here for any application for a job I might make. I am beginning to think that the sooner I'm away from here the better.'

'I know that neurosurgery is a high-risk speciality,' Sinclair said, 'and I wonder if you can recall any major problem with a patient under Kershaw's care recently which might have led to ill feeling or worse with the relatives.'

Fielding thought for a moment or two, then nodded. 'Yes, there was one case only a few weeks ago that caused me a great deal of worry. It concerned a young woman who had had a subarachnoid haemorrhage from an aneurysm on one of the arteries of the brain. I won't go into every detail; suffice it to say that there is what amounts to a weakness in the wall of the artery and the patient is usually quite unaware of it until the blood leaks out. If the haemorrhage is catastrophic, the patient dies suddenly, but if there is merely a leak, the patient may retain consciousness and be able to complain of the sudden onset of a very severe headache. In the latter case, surgery needs to be undertaken very soon after the incident, as the risk of a fatal recurrence of the bleeding is high.

'Depending on the site of the aneurysm, surgery may be anything from relatively simple to a nightmare. In this particular case, the aneurysm was on the anterior communicating artery, one of the easier sites to access, and Kershaw was able to clip it quickly and encountered no particular problems during the operation. Initially, the patient did extremely well, but two weeks later, while in our convalescent home, she died suddenly from a pulmonary embolus.'

'Yes, I know about that. It's a blood clot detaching from a vein, usually in the legs, which lodges in the lungs, isn't it?

The man nodded. 'Yes, that's right. We knew that the young woman had been on the pill, which increases the risk of it happening, but even in that situation it is a rare occurrence, particularly in someone young, who has spent quite a short time in the operating theatre and who was not confined to bed afterwards for more than twenty-four hours. In any case, the incidence of pulmonary embolus in Kershaw's practice was significantly lower than that with any of the other neurosurgeons here and I have no doubt that that was due to his brilliant technique and the speed with which he operated.'

'And in the case you've described, there was trouble with the relatives?'

'There certainly was, mainly with the patient's husband. Kershaw refused to see him, which I think was most unwise as it undoubtedly fuelled the man's anger. I got the whole works. Kershaw hadn't taken proper care of his wife; he was directly responsible for her death and hadn't even had the common decency to face him and apologize and he threatened legal action against Kershaw for negligence.

'Of course, I did my best to explain to the man that his wife had only hours to live had surgery not taken place and that we knew she had been on the pill, which added to the risk of blood clots after surgery with the danger of pulmonary emboli. We had done everything possible to minimize the risk of a pulmonary embolus. She had had physiotherapy to the legs, which is where most blood clots originate, and she was mobilized as quickly as possible. Mr Kershaw had operated without any delay and his technique was such that she was on the operating table for a relatively short time, another reason why the incidence of pulmonary emboli in his cases was lower that that of any of the other surgeons in the hospital.'

'And presumably your detailed explanation didn't work.'

'No, I'm afraid that it didn't and although the man didn't actually deliver any threats, he was very direct and uncompromising about what he said about Kershaw.'

'In what way, exactly?'

'That he should be struck off and put in prison for gross negligence, but even that wouldn't be enough.'

'Did he go as far as to threaten to kill him?'

'Not in so many words, but I have to say that I found his attitude very worrying – he was completely out of control.'

'I presume you told Kershaw about it.'

'Yes, I did, and all he did was to thank me for dealing with the man and tell me that people were liable to behave like that when they were under severe stress, as if I wasn't well aware of that already. He finished by saying that he was sure that the man would come to terms with what had happened in due course and that I mustn't worry about it.'

'Did Kershaw appear to be concerned about the situation himself?'

'Not in the least. He merely told me not to get so het up about it and that incidents like that were an occupational hazard of a speciality like ours.'

'Were there any further repercussions?'

'No, but I felt I had to report the whole business to my medical defence organization and they suggested that I wrote down all that had happened and the details of my conversation with the husband and to tell Kershaw what I had done.'

'And you did?'

'Yes.'

'And his reaction?'

'He just said that people under stress said intemperate things on the spur of the moment, that most of them were well aware that surgery inside the skull carried risks with it, and that I should not take incidents like that so much to heart.'

'What did you make of that?'

'I thought that what he had said was unfeeling and completely beside the point. If the man had acknowledged the efforts I had made to calm the wretched husband of that patient down, I'm sure I would have accepted that he was unable to face that sort of situation himself and handling those situations for him was part of my job. But for him to pass it off as being a matter of little consequence made me realize that I needed to be my own man and that I should get away from both Kershaw and this hospital as soon as a good opportunity presented itself.'

'But surely you must have faced similar situations often enough before?'

'Yes, but never in quite such distressing circumstances or with such an extreme reaction from a patient's husband or wife. To be honest, in the past I had been flattered to be given the responsibility for dealing with relatives pre- and post-operatively, knowing that I had the ability to do it well, but for Kershaw to dismiss my upset and concern in that particular instance so casually made me realize that I had had enough of working with him. Don't get me wrong. I had enjoyed most of my time with him. I was grateful for his tuition and the opportunity to be able to watch a very special talent at close quarters and I am well aware that without that experience I wouldn't be half the surgeon I am now.'

'Did you tell your wife about that case?'

'No, I didn't. My job was already causing strains in our marriage and I don't blame her for that. Life couldn't have been easy for her and I should have realized long before I did that she was bored and, being so bound up with my work, which was extremely tiring and stressful, I failed to understand just how fed up she must have been and how little time I was spending with her.'

'Did you mention any of this to Kershaw?'

'Yes, I did, a few months ago. To my surprise, he listened carefully to what I had to say, said that Annette ought to get a job and if she was able to find something here, that would be a bonus as we would be able to meet during the day. He asked if she had taken 'A' levels, and when I told him that she had obtained decent grades in chemistry and biology he told me that he had been thinking about her doing a secretarial training, but, in view of that, suggested that Annette should try for a training job as a technician in the electrophysiology department, which he had heard was about to be

135

advertised. I don't know what strings he pulled, if any, but she got the job. She took to it straight away and what with that and the visit to the sex counsellor, she became a different person, becoming cheerful and enthusiastic.

'With our combined salaries, we were able to afford a cleaner, who proved to be excellent; she keeps the flat immaculate, does the shopping and leaves our evening meals in the fridge. I can't tell you what a difference all this has made to our marriage.'

'Did you ever socialize with Kershaw and his family?'

'Just the once when Lady Elizabeth invited us to dinner not all that long ago. That was a truly dreadful occasion as far as I was concerned, but Annette carried it off brilliantly. She even told me off afterwards for being too obsequious! When we relived it later, with devastating effect, she imitated their extraordinary manservant, Kershaw's intense daughter and his stiff and regal wife. The only bit of light relief was Lady Elizabeth's brother, who did his best to lighten the atmosphere. Annette was also obviously a hit with Kershaw as I could see them talking animatedly throughout the meal.

'What gave me much needed relief after dinner was Kershaw's daughter, Alison, who must have realized how out of place I felt and as a result suggested that I might be interested to see Kershaw's workshop, where he did his wood carving. Not only was I mightily impressed by what I saw but, on her own, I found Alison to be both well informed and interesting.

'As for Annette, she could hardly have failed to realize how uneasy and embarrassed I had been throughout the whole evening, and when we returned home she told me that I had taken the whole thing far too seriously and that it was time I stopped kowtowing to Kershaw and stood up for myself for a change. She pointed out that the food and drink was first rate and that I should have done what she did, which was to relax and enjoy it. She was quite right, of course. There was I thinking that she would be out of place in that environment, whereas she had clearly revelled in it and really sparkled. I was very proud of her for the way she had carried it off. You see, she used to be so shy and diffident, even apart from the sex thing, but in the preceding few months she has become really confident in herself and much more outgoing. I put most of that down to her doing so well in her new job, which has brought her right out of her shell.'

'I have to ask you what you were doing on the Sunday afternoon when Kershaw was murdered.'

'Of course. I understand that. I was on call as I usually was at weekends apart from holidays and the odd one when one of the senior registrars on the other firms covered for me, and on those occasions Kershaw was always available on his pager. All that afternoon, I was in the flat at the hospital working on a paper I hope to get published soon.'

'Was your wife with you that afternoon?'

'No. She was down in the Isle of Wight that weekend, staying with her parents.'

'Were you aware that Kershaw was in the habit of working at his woodwork on Sunday afternoons?'

'Not until his daughter told me about it when she took me up to his workshop after that dinner.'

'So you didn't even know that it was on the floor above the garage until that day?'

'No. Kershaw and I didn't have that sort of relationship and he never said anything to me about his private life away from the hospital.'

'How did you communicate with him if there was a problem at the hospital at weekends or at night?'

'Always through his mobile phone.'

Kershaw's golf club was not all that far from the house in Highgate and Sinclair went down there that afternoon. The secretary, one Major Findlay, looked to be in his late fifties and was wearing a black blazer, cavalry twill trousers, brilliantly polished brown shoes and a regimental tie.

'Yes,' he said when Sinclair had introduced himself, 'of course I knew Richard Kershaw. He was a member here for many years, long before I was appointed as secretary, and used to play a round most Sunday mornings with Graham Robertson, one of our stalwarts, who was captain a few years back.

'I often used to watch them when they came up the eighteenth at about ten. They liked to get off as early as possible because both of them, particularly Kershaw, liked to play quickly. He couldn't be doing with fourballs and the fiddle-faddle of testing the direction of the wind, agonizing over which club to take and stalking the greens and surveying the line of each putt from every conceivable angle. For him and Robertson, it was one quick look, a club pulled out of the bag with hardly more than a glance up the fairway and no practice swings. More often than not, there was a sharp click and the ball would go off in a graceful arc, usually straight.

'It was a joy to watch them and I'm not even sure that they kept the score. On the eighteenth green there was always a smile, a brief handshake and, after a shower and a quick cup of coffee, away he went.'

'Did you know him well yourself?'

'No, but he always gave me a nod and a smile whenever we passed each other in the clubhouse, but, as Robertson explained to me, the man was far too busy to get involved in committee work and he was never available for matches. That was a sore point with the current captain, because Kershaw was one of our better players with a handicap of six.'

'Would it be possible for me to have a word with Mr Robertson?'

'I don't see why not. He's a widower with no children and he spends a great deal of his time here. He's probably having a post-lunch cup of coffee in the members' lounge now. I'll see if he's there and, if he is, you're welcome to use my office for a quiet chat. I'm due to walk round the course with the head groundsman shortly and you won't be disturbed in there. My secretary will field any phone calls in the outer office.'

'Thank you, you've been most helpful.

The man inclined his head slightly. 'The news of Kershaw's death came as a great shock to me and indeed to all our members. I didn't know him at all well, but he was a most agreeable man and always happy to have a word whenever our paths crossed. I am also well aware what a great loss he is to medicine.'

Graham Robertson was an alert, athletic-looking

man in his middle fifties, who smiled when Sinclair explained that he was working on the murder enquiry as one of Roger Tyrrell's team.

'Yes,' he said, 'I remember meeting Tyrrell at the Halford Hewitt a few years back. Nice man and an excellent golfer. Now, how may I help you?'

'Naturally, we have been making extensive enquiries about Kershaw, both at his home and at the hospital, but we would also like to know more about his leisure activities. I saw his Callaways at his house and discovered that he was a member here and the secretary mentioned your name as someone who knew him well and was his regular opponent early on Sunday mornings.'

'Yes and I miss him more than I can say. I knew him for more than twenty years and played innumerable Sunday games with him.'

'Did he seem any different that morning before he was killed?'

'No, not at all. Richard had a high-revving engine inside him – the shrinks would no doubt call him mildly hypomanic – and that morning he was his usual self. It was accepted that unless there was a match or a competition, the two of us would be allowed to go off first, the simple reason being that we played so quickly. Invariably we were round in under two and a half hours and we enjoyed the brisk exercise almost as much as the golf. Richard could have been really good had he practised more and his approach had been less cavalier, but advising that was worse than useless.'

'Did the two of you talk much on the course?'

'Yes, but only when each of us had weighed up the

shot required and played it. His golfing manners in that respect were impeccable.'

'What did you talk about?'

'Anything except work and family matters.'

'Why not family matters?'

'Perhaps it's a bit of a class thing – I feel the same way about it myself. There is, of course, a time and a place for that sort of conversation, but a golf course is not one of them.'

'Would you say that Kershaw was a happy man?'

'Without any shadow of a doubt. He radiated it. If I felt down about anything, a round of golf with him was always enough to dispel my mood completely for a couple of hours or so and afterwards I was often able to view my concerns in a much calmer light.'

'What about his health?'

'His whole manner exuded well-being and energy and you only had to see him in the shower room after our game to realize that. Curiously, though, in that situation he always liked to guard his modesty, invariably using one of the only two closed showers and coming out with a towel round his middle.'

'Why curiously?'

'Almost everyone I knew with his background of public school and high-level sport at university is so used to walking about naked in changing rooms after games that I would have expected him to do the same. Certainly it never occurs to all of those here with that background, including myself, to do anything else.'

'Why do you suppose he was modest like that?'

'I have no real idea. Some anatomical peculiarity, perhaps.'

141

He had an anatomical peculiarity, all right, after those caning sessions, Sinclair thought, and it was only the Friday before his death that he had had a particularly vigorous version of his preferred sexual variation. No wonder he didn't wish to show the results to either his friend or the other members of the club.

'Did you ever meet his wife and children?'

'No, nor did we ever discuss them. Now you mention it, it reminds me of my time in the army, when religion, sex and one's family were taboo subjects in the mess.'

'What about work?'

'It was never mentioned by either of us. Those Sunday mornings were a time of relaxation and of good golf. Make no mistake about it, though, both of us tried to win and that, in my opinion, is how it should be.'

'Did you play on the morning of the Sunday on which he was killed?'

'Yes, we did. I remember seeing the news in the paper on the Tuesday after it happened.'

'Was he his usual self?'

'He certainly was. In excellent form.'

'Was Kershaw a good loser?'

'Exemplary. Win or lose, a handshake, an engaging grin and a "well played" were all either of us said about the round. There were never any complaints of bad luck, recriminations or excuses and "if onlys". He just radiated pleasure at a good contest with a like-minded opponent. All right, so there was no depth to our friendship, but that was the point. What we had together was pure relaxed enjoyment.'

'I know that Kershaw got a hockey blue at Oxford. Did he play golf seriously there, as well?'

'No, he didn't. With hockey and the demands of his medical course, he didn't have enough time to devote to doing that as well other than with an occasional purely recreational round, mostly in the vacations.'

'Well, thank you. That gave me a very clear picture of what Kershaw was like on the golf course, and what an attractive one it was, too. He doesn't sound the sort of fellow to have made enemies.'

'After having spent many years in the army and been in a number of distinctly sticky situations such as the Falklands and Northern Ireland, I like to think that I am a reasonably good judge of people's character, and I wouldn't have thought so. However, I only saw him under the particular set of circumstances I have described and all I can say is that he was one of the most engaging people I have ever met.'

'Thank you again. You have made that very clear and I am most grateful.'

The man smiled. 'I must say that your being a fellow golfer made my task much easier. Yes, I am obsessed with useless sporting information, but on this occasion it proved extremely useful. You see, I know that you played in the President's Putter. I didn't go to Oxbridge myself, but I happened to be staying with a friend near Rye some years ago. We went to watch it and it was then that I saw you play. Should you ever feel like a relaxing game, you only have to let me know.'

'Would that I were able to do so,' Sinclair replied. 'There are many times when I agree with Gilbert's assessment of "the policeman's lot" and this is one of them, particularly as it is such a high-profile case involving such a well-known man, and the press also

143

has to be taken into account. Recreation, even on a Sunday, would no doubt provoke adverse comment. However, when all this settles down, I would like nothing better than to take up your kind offer.'

CHAPTER SEVEN

Sarah Prescott found Annette Fielding in the applied neurophysiology department of the hospital.

'I won't be able to talk to you just now,' the young woman said after Sarah had explained that she knew that she had been to dinner at the Kershaw's house and she was trying to get a feel for the sort of man he was by speaking to as many people, who had met him, as possible. 'I'm about to sit in on an investigation, which I'll have to do on my own in the near future and I can't afford to miss out on that. Why don't we sit in the garden in the middle of the square after I've finished with it and I've had a quick swim with Rebecca Cochrane. Twelve to one is the only time we're allowed to use the nurses' pool and it's strictly for the female members of the staff, but not that many ever seem to take advantage of it. You're very welcome to join us there, but I'm afraid I won't be able to lend you a costume – my other one's at home – and anyway, it would annoy Rebecca. Your being there at all will do that anyway and that'll be no bad thing.

'Your presence should dampen her ardour, if nothing else will, and she might even get the message that I'm not that way inclined. Just because we were chatting one day and I told her that I got fed up at times with the amount of time John spent in the operating theatre, she seemed to think that I needed to be rescued and comforted in more ways than one.

'You won't believe this, but I thought she was just being friendly the first time she suggested that we had a swim together because she was very careful not to hint that she might be interested in me in more ways than one. Recently, though, I have caught her looking at me, or a certain part of me, more directly than was appropriate and she asked me if I was lonely with John working all hours. I must confess that to some extent it was my fault. You see, having been to an all-girls boarding school, I had got used to wandering around with nothing on – we all did – and when I came out of the shower cubicle the other day and started to dry myself in front of her, the penny dropped with a loud clang.

'Rebecca couldn't take her eyes off you know where. She hasn't tried anything on yet, but I'm sure she'd like to and your presence should act as a cold shower and give me the opportunity to put a stop to it. I should, of course, have given her the brush-off straight away, but I knew that she was almost certain to get the consultant job in cardiology here, which indeed she did a few weeks later, and I thought that if I made a great issue out of it, it might prejudice John's chances of promotion.

'Anyway, once she sees you down there, it should give her the frighteners and cool things down a bit.'

Sarah wasn't at all sure that it would be wise to get

caught up in a situation involving Rebecca Cochrane's sexual preference, nor was it at all clear what Annette Fielding had in mind to do at the swimming pool. In the end, though, the need to find out more about Annette overcame any reservations and, during the lunch break, she followed her into the nurses' hostel and down the stairs to the basement swimming pool.

'Why not sit on that bench over there while I get changed,' Annette said.

She reappeared from the cubicle a few minutes later wearing a one piece swimsuit, cut high up on her thighs and, after putting her towel on the bench, sat down beside the detective.

'I suggest we continue our chat after the swim. Rebecca is a stickler for punctuality and she's bound to arrive any minute now.'

Sarah nodded. 'How's the electrophysiology going?'

'Not too badly. I'm really getting into it now. I found some of them in the department pretty impatient with me to start with and I felt inhibited about asking them simple questions. That's absolutely no problem with my husband and he is very good at explaining things. He also pushes me and is quite demanding, which is just what I need. There's no slacking with him, I can tell you.'

'How well did you know Mr Kershaw?'

At that moment, Rebecca came in through the door and she flushed slightly when she saw Sarah sitting there.

'The Inspector here wanted to have a word with me and she very kindly offered to wait until after we'd had our swim.' Annette said.

Sarah saw Rebecca Cochrane frown and then the young woman turned, moved swiftly into the cubicle and emerged a few minutes later in her swim suit, which was a good deal more modest than that of the other young woman.

Lips held tightly together and throwing her towel down without looking in their direction, Rebecca went into the pool in a flat dive and began to churn up and down in a fast crawl, doing tumble turns at each end. Annette raised her eyebrows slightly as she looked at Sarah, then descended the ladder and, keeping close to the side of the pool, set off in a decorous breast stroke. Rebecca came out of the water first, rinsed herself quickly under the open shower at the side of the pool, still wearing her costume, and then disappeared into the cubicle, while the other young woman continued to swim slowly up and down.

When she emerged from the water, Annette Fielding stripped off her bathing costume and, making no attempt to cover herself, moved towards the open shower just as Rebecca, now fully dressed, emerged from the cubicle.

She stopped dead in her tracks as she saw the naked young woman, flushed and then looked across at Sarah.

'I'll leave you two to have a chat,' she said. 'See you tomorrow, Annette.'

'I'm afraid that I won't be able to swim with you again for the time being, Rebecca. You see, John is hardly operating at all at present and we have a lot to discuss. There is his future, which may have to be away from here, and he is under great stress as the result of what happened to Mr Kershaw. John badly needs my support and at long last it looks as if he'll be able to take a proper break every lunchtime and I need to be there for him.'

Sarah saw Rebecca Cochrane press her lips tightly together, then, without saying a word, the young woman strode out through the door towards the stairs.

'I should have done that long ago,' Annette said, turning to face Sarah. 'I'll just have my shower and then perhaps we could have our chat outside in the garden in the square. It should be warm enough.'

After she had finished in the shower, she took a few steps back towards Sarah, picked up her towel and dried herself before going back into the cubicle to get dressed.

'Right,' she said when she came out, 'I'll just dump this stuff in my locker on the way out.'

There was an unoccupied bench in the garden opposite the main entrance to the hospital and they sat side by side under the shelter of a tree.

'How well did you know Richard Kershaw?' Sarah asked.

'Hardly at all. Most of the consultants don't socialize with their junior staff and Kershaw was no exception. The fact that he did ask John and me to dinner at his house a few weeks ago was more than most of the others did. I have to confess that I was more than a bit anxious about it beforehand, but that evening was quite something, I can tell you.

'First of all there was that creepy manservant, who looked like a refugee from one of those pre-war films that they dredge up on TV from time to time. In a black suit, he inclined his head when he had opened the front door to let us in and in his ever so proper and precise voice said: "Good evening sir, madam. May I take your coats?"

'It was obvious to me that Kershaw was going to milk the situation for all it was worth. He shook John warmly by the hand and then turned to me with a smile and said: "and you must be the lady wife. It is a pleasure to meet you and I am delighted that you were able to come."

'The whole evening could have been excruciating and I'm afraid that John found it just that, but I enjoyed every minute of it. Kershaw was such fun and easy to talk to and there was the forbidding Lady Elizabeth, of whom John was clearly terrified. Her brother looked nothing like her and did his best to engage both John and his sister in light conversation, and then there was Kershaw's daughter. She was very quietly spoken and said very little to John during dinner, but afterwards, to my relief, she must have noticed how embarrassed he was, not least by the stiff Lady Elizabeth, and she took him off to have a look at Kershaw's workshop. John told me afterwards how impressed he had been by what he saw. He also said how nice Kershaw's daughter had been. I asked John if he fancied her and that was a great mistake. John never did have much of a sense of humour and was quite upset, even when I told him that it had just been a joke.

'I have to say that after the two of them had gone up to the workshop, the whole atmosphere lightened and Lady Elizabeth's brother kept us entertained with some rather good stories and I was also able to have a quite chat with our hostess. To my surprise, I found her rather nice, not at all the great lady, and she was obviously interested to know how I was getting on with marriage to a highly driven and work-obsessed husband.

' "I can tell you," she said, "that I know all about that, but it has many compensations and I'm sure you'll find the same when your husband gets a consultant post. I hesitate to give you advice, my dear, but what I found was that once the children were older and I had some time to myself, the answer proved to be finding a career for myself. True, it has been almost entirely voluntary work, but that was and is extremely rewarding and may be you'll find the same in a field suitable for your talents."

'There was a good deal of sense in what she said and I told her about the training post in clinical neurophysiology that I had just started.

' "Good for you," she said. "I'm sure you'll never regret it and, who knows, you may want to go back to it later, should you decide to have children."

'I rather liked the way she put that, quite unlike my mother, who has always assumed that children were a matter of when, not if, and she is always getting at me about it.'

'And the job's working out well?'

'Yes, it is and it has helped my marriage, too. I have been able to appreciate what John is doing in a much more informed way and I had become bored with being on my own so much. He has also been very generous with his time in helping me so much. He has a real gift for explaining in simple language concepts which I found difficult to understand at first and that, too, has brought us together.'

'And, from what you've just said, I imagine that you have put the question of a family on hold for the time being.'

'Yes, that's right. If and when are difficult questions for us at present and with a career such as yours, I'm sure you understand all about the pros and cons. Once John gets a consultant post, though, we'll give the matter serious thought and make a decision then.'

'Presumably your husband goes along with that.'

'He certainly does and in a funny sort of way the tragic death of Richard Kershaw has given us both a wake-up call.'

'In what way?'

'It has made me realize that our marriage had been heading for the rocks. John had become totally obsessed with his work, so much so that I was beginning to wonder if I had a proper husband or some sort of automaton controlled by Kershaw, the puppet master. Of course I realized that John's future was very dependent on the man, but enough was enough and I'm sorry to say that I was becoming more and more critical and, let's face it, shrewish.

'It has been an enormous relief for me to hear John talking about getting a consultant post right away from here, where he can be his own man and be a husband as well as a neurosurgeon. It won't be all that long before I qualify as a clinical neurophysiology technician and we have both agreed to postpone a family until we know where and under what circumstances we will be living. If he gets a job outside London, John thinks that the chances of my finding something in the field in which I am now working will be good and a plus for him if and when he applies for a post in the provinces. If that works out, it would also be something I could go back to once our family is complete.'

'And Rebecca Cochrane?'

'That was my fault. I first met her at a party here about eighteen months ago, when John introduced me to her – at that time she was a senior registrar – and they had been students together in the same year at St Gregory's. She seemed nice enough, obviously realized that I was lonely, particularly if John was operating at weekends and we did a few things together. John was very much hoping to get a consultant post here – Kershaw had hinted that he might be able to persuade the powers that be to enlarge his firm and John would make the ideal partner – and it seemed a good idea to try to get Rebecca, who was the overwhelming favourite to get a consultant post in cardiology when the senior man retired in a few months from that time, to back John. That's why I decided to get friendly with her.

'Anyway, I used to meet Rebecca for lunch on the occasional Saturday if John was busy and it was she who suggested that I should try for the post in the electrophysiology department. She knew one of the consultants in it well and there is no doubt that her influence helped me to get the post. It wasn't until we started to swim together in the lunch hour that I realized that she also had another agenda. She started to give me chaste kisses each time we met and then gradually it became a bit more than that. Stupidly, I decided to provoke her to see how far she might go. As you saw, I started taking off my swimming costume in that open shower by the pool and then going into the changing room without bothering to wrap my towel about me.

'Only recently did I realize that the whole thing was getting out of control, that I was playing with fire and behaving badly. When you wanted to interview me, I suggested that you come down to the pool as it seemed a good opportunity both to embarrass her even more, and warn her off. I realize that I was very stupid not to have realized what she was up to a long time ago and should have been careful not to have given her the impression that I was interested in her sexually. Anyway, from her reaction just now, it looks as if she has got the message at last.'

'Have you mentioned any of this to your husband?'

'John is rather prudish and I just knew that he wouldn't be able to take anything like that in his stride and I very much regret now that I was stupid enough to have got involved with Rebecca in the first place. The only excuse I can put forward is that I was lonely and bored at the time it all started.'

'How do you view a possible move out of London, which I gather is a possibility with the neurosurgical job coming up in the South.'

'I look forward to it.'

'I hope everything goes well for you, but a word of warning. It is in everyone's interest here that we track down Richard Kershaw's killer as soon as possible and it is vitally important that no important information about him or his relationships with the staff is withheld from us, and that includes both you and your husband.'

The young woman turned her head and looked Sarah

straight in the eye. 'Yes, we both realize that and only the other day I overhead someone hinting that Kershaw's death had come at a very convenient time for John, which was a terrible thing to say.'

The following morning, the two detectives met Tyrrell in his office.

'So you've no doubt, Sarah, that Kershaw's plaything and Fielding's wife are one and the same person,' he said after his two assistants had given him accounts of their various interviews.

'None at all, sir. If what Fielding told Mark about his wife being shy and inexperienced before she started to work at the hospital is true, then she's the very reverse of that now. You should have seen the way she paraded around naked when taking her shower by the swimming pool. I realize that the reason she put forward was that she wanted to embarrass Rebecca Cochrane, but there was more to it than that. She was enjoying herself and to some extent trying to do the same thing to me. I also have no doubt at all about her being the woman playing games with Kershaw. The shape of her body, her height and gait all convinced me that she was the one.

'It was also only too obvious that Rebecca Cochrane was very put out by the way that Annette behaved at the pool and I had a further word with her after she had finished her clinic that afternoon. She told me that when they first met, Annette seemed shy and very lonely and that was why she befriended her. They got on very well at first, but all that began to change about a year ago. She started to become much more animated and the very reverse of shy at the pool. I doubt very much if they ever had a physical relationship, but I am convinced that Rebecca is gay and tries hard to hide it and probably also does her best to suppress it. I felt the same about her when we were investigating her father's murder.

'Be that as it may, the change in Annette's behaviour fits in with the time she started to play games with Kershaw in the flat.'

'Do you think that that transformation is credible?'

'I have no reason not to, sir. I've seen it before with seemingly meek and mild young women changing completely once they've got involved with the wilder manifestations of sex.'

'Right. I'd like to have a talk to that young woman myself with you in attendance, Sarah, and perhaps Kershaw's flat would be the right place and some time tomorrow would suit me best, provided we are able to persuade the industrious Miss Perry to take some time off.

'Mark, would you have a word with the husband of that woman who died following surgery a few weeks ago? He seems to have lost control completely when his wife died and he has to be a suspect, although I think rather a long shot. After all, whoever did murder Kershaw must have been very conversant with his activities on Sunday afternoons and it seems to me unlikely that this man, Morley, would have been able to find out about them without stalking him for some time. Fielding is still in the frame and perhaps a check on his activities that Sunday afternoon would also be worthwhile.'

'Very well, sir, I'll get onto it straight away.'

As Sinclair had expected, there was no reply from the phone number that Miss Perry had given him and the address proved to be in Fulham, not far from Parsons Green undeground station, only two stops from their own local station, East Putney.

'I'll give him another ring early this evening,' he said to Sarah when they were on their way back to her flat.

'Would you like me to come with you to provide a bit of moral support?'

Sinclair looked across at his partner, who was driving.

'Worried that I might get upset when we start talking about subarachnoid haemorrhages?'

'Yes. I know, of course, that your wife's sudden death from the same condition occurred under very different circumstances, but I'm still worried that talking to this man might be very upsetting for you.'

'Thanks to you, Sarah, I've long since come to terms with what happened to my wife and this case is very different. The death of Morley's wife was very clearly related to the operation and he may well feel that it must have been someone's fault and that there is a conspiracy of silence concerning it, particularly with Kershaw having refused to meet him. Fielding obviously did his best with the man, but if he still feels bitter and angry, my own experience may make it easier for me to get him to talk about it and maybe even reassure him that it was no one's fault.'

'Always provided, of course, that he didn't decide to take revenge out on Kershaw,' Sarah said. Sinclair nodded and gave her a smile. 'As usual, you have hit the nail firmly on the head and I'll bear that very much in mind when I see him. It was very sweet of you to offer to come with me, but I think that a one-to-one chat is likely to appear less threatening and thus more productive.'

Brian Morley was in when Sinclair rang his number in Fulham early that evening and agreed to see him at nine. He proved to be a very large young man, who looked to be in his middle twenties.

'Let me say straight away,' he said when the two of them were in the sitting room and Sinclair had introduced himself, 'that I am not in the last surprised that you have come to see me. There is no doubt that I behaved very badly after Rachel's death. You see it was the most appalling roller coaster ride. She and I had not been married for very long, no more than six months, and let me just say that during that time we had been blissfully happy. There is no point in beating about the bush, because I was quite frank about what had happened when I saw Mr Fielding at St Gregory's Hospital, directly after he had assessed her condition in the casualty department there.

'I told him that we had been having, how shall I put it, enthusiastic sex late that Sunday afternoon, when quite suddenly she let out a cry and was just able to tell me that she had had a sudden blinding headache. She never lost consciousness completely and was moaning with pain. I shall never forget the way she looked; it was easily the most distressing experience of my life.

'I couldn't fault the ambulance people. They arrived

within fifteen minutes of my 999 call, seemed to know at once that she had had a brain haemorrhage, and they got her to St Gregory's within thirty minutes of their arrival.

'I also found the senior registrar in neurosurgery there, John Fielding, wonderfully reassuring. He explained that Rachel had had a subarachnoid haemorrhage. In simple terms, he then told me that it had occurred because there had been a weakness in the wall of one of the arteries in the brain, very probably since birth, that that had allowed a swelling to take place and that blood had leaked out, which was the cause of the severe headache. He went on to say that the event could not have been predicted and that tests would have to be done to pinpoint the exact site of the weakness and the extent of any damage. He then told me that it was quite likely that an operation would be possible to repair the artery and, if so, Mr Kershaw, one of the neurosurgeons, who was generally recognized to be the best man in that field in the country, would be called in.

'I was amazed by how well it went and directly she came round from the anaesthetic, my wife was able to say a few words to me.' The man shook his head. 'It was some two weeks later, when she was already at the convalescent home, that quite suddenly, without any warning, she died. I have to confess that I lost control completely. I demanded to see the surgeon who had carried out the operation and when that was turned down, I shouted out that I was going to deal with him once and for all.

'Mr Fielding, who had to take the brunt of my

uncontrolled rage, during which I issued the most ridiculous threats, was absolutely brilliant.'

'What sort of threats?'

'Oh, that I was going to get my revenge on Kershaw, that killing him would be too good for him and that by the time I had finished with him, he'd wish he'd never been born.

'Fielding seemed to realize that I didn't mean it and waited until I had calmed down a bit and then said: "I know just how difficult this must be for you, but first I would like you to listen carefully to what I have to say without interruption and then feel absolutely free to ask any questions you like and make notes if that would help you." His manner and voice were so gentle and understanding that to my later surprise, when I came to think about it, I was able to do what he suggested.

' "I've already explained how this haemorrhage came to take place," he said "and how sometimes it is fatal at the time, also that the likelihood of a recurrence with disastrous results, is very high. In your wife's case, the diagnosis was made immediately after her arrival at the hospital. A special X-ray, called an arteriogram, identified the exact site of the problem and it was dealt with by arguably the most skilful surgeon in that field in the country.

"The immediate result was highly satisfactory and you were able to talk to your wife very soon after she came round from the anaesthetic. The excellent progress continued and within a few days she was up and about and a week later went to our convalescent home, where, ten days later, she so sadly died suddenly from a pulmonary embolus."

'He went on to explain that a blood clot in a vein, usually in the legs, is a well-known complication of any form of surgery and if it flies off and lodges in the lungs, sudden death may occur. He told me that the incidence of this complication in Mr Kershaw's cases, and the outcome of the surgery that my wife underwent, was probably better than in any other published figures and that that was due to his manual dexterity and speed of action. The risk of a pulmonary embolus occurring was lower in young people, but in my wife's case, the contraceptive pills that she had been taking may well have been a contributory factor.

'I asked him what steps had been take to prevent it from happening and he told me that the use of anticoagulant drugs was not possible after arterial surgery and that coming off the pill, physiotherapy to the legs and as short a time as possible in bed was the best way of avoiding it, and that was exactly what had been organized in Rachel's case.

'Finally, I asked him why a junior doctor had been delegated to see me and not the surgeon who had operated.'

'How did he respond to that?'

'He pointed out that, as he had already explained, he was not a junior doctor, that he had been assisting Mr Kershaw and carrying out surgery on the brain independently for five years, and that he expected to become a consultant in the very near future. He told me that Kershaw did what he did best, which was to operate, and that he found other parts of medicine, particularly meeting relatives, intolerably stressful and

161

that he delegated that whenever possible.

'Fielding finished up by suggesting that I study the extensive notes, which he had made in order to help me understand what had happened. Finally, he said that if I felt that I needed to discuss it with someone else privately and away from St Gregory's Hospital, he would be happy to recommend an appropriate surgeon with extensive experience of the condition. He warned me that that would inevitably involve me in considerable expense, but should I decide to do so, he would arrange for copies of the notes and X-rays to be forwarded as appropriate. Finally, he told me that he was always available if I had any further questions after I had read his notes and had thought it all over in detail.'

'And did you get a second opinion?'

'Yes, I did, and I chose the only woman who was on the list of neurosurgeons who was prepared to act in that way and she confirmed everything that Fielding had told me. I must confess that after that, by which time I had calmed down, I felt ashamed of my aggression towards the man and decided to apologise in person.'

'How did he react?'

'He said that he fully understood my anger and thanked me for finally being so understanding. That was, in fact, a travesty of the truth; I had been both rude to him and insulting. I believe, though, that he hadn't taken umbrage at all and his concern for my distress was completely genuine.'

'In the light of all of that, what is your view of Kershaw now?'

'The other neurosurgeon, whom I consulted, virtually reiterated what Fielding had said about him. As a technician, she said, Kershaw was the very best there was, but one had to accept that he had serious shortcomings as a manager of people. I still find that impossible to understand. How can a man who carries out any form of surgery, let alone on peoples' brains, divorce himself completely from the human side of what he is doing?'

'You might like to consider how much people's expectations have changed with regard to surgery and for medicine as a whole, for that matter,' Sinclair said. 'It was not all that long ago, in my parents' generation, say, when it was assumed that doctors and surgeons, in particular, were doing their best. If something went wrong, even if the patient died, their immediate assumption was not that someone had been negligent; they realized that surgery of any kind, particularly on the brain, was a very risky business indeed and that there was a danger of death. Now, people's first reaction is that there has been carelessness of some sort. I have personal experience of the condition that your wife had and its tragic outcome myself, and I have also discussed your wife's case with an independent expert and I am convinced that no mistakes were made. As to Kershaw's inability to communicate with patients or their relatives, it is surely better to accept one's shortcomings in that regard than to do it badly and make oneself anxious in the operating theatre, perhaps dwelling on how terrible it would be if things went wrong rather than concentrating on the job in hand. Anyhow, that's something that's not directly to do with me and is up to you to think about further.

'One last thing. You do realize, don't you, that I have to ask you what you were doing on the Sunday afternoon when Kershaw was murdered?'

The man nodded. 'I'm not an avid follower of the news, either in the papers or on TV, and you'll have to tell me when it occurred.'

Sinclair observed Morley very carefully while he was leafing through his diary and his expression didn't alter.

'I already knew that this wouldn't be helpful. I was given three weeks compassionate leave by my firm when Rachel died and I was fully occupied by the funeral arrangements and family matters. After I went back to work, at weekends, I've tried to get the flat into shape, doing some housework and washing and, on the Sunday afternoon you mentioned, I might well have been dozing during an attempt to do the crossword and I very likely had the cricket on TV. Don't ask me who was playing; it was just a background.'

'How did you get on?' Sarah asked when he got back to the flat.

'Not too badly. In fact, I was rather impressed by this fellow, Morley. He freely admitted that he had lost it completely immediately after his wife's death, but when he had obtained a second opinion on all that had happened, he calmed down. I believe that he has genuinely accepted that the tragedy had not been Kershaw's fault and that a pulmonary embolus was a recognized risk of any form of surgery and that everything practical had been done to try to prevent it.

He says he was in his flat, dozing and half watching TV on the afternoon of Kershaw's murder and he didn't come up with a fancy alibi for that time, and I also found that convincing, as he made no attempt to make it overelaborate.

'Fielding comes out of this very well. He clearly was able to calm the man down and it was he who suggested the second opinion and arranged for notes and X-rays to be forwarded to the surgeon in question.'

CHAPTER EIGHT

Sarah Prescott was waiting in the front hall of the hospital when Annette Fielding came hurrying through the door just before eight-thirty the following morning.

'I can't stop now,' the young woman said when the detective got up from her chair and approached her. 'I'm due to start an investigation at nine o'clock and I need to check all the equipment.'

'That's all right. Chief Superintendent Tyrrell would like a word with you during your lunch hour.'

'But, as I told you, that's when I've been meeting John recently.'

'You'll have to give that a miss today. This is far more important. I'll meet you here at twelve-thirty – I understand that that's when you're normally free.'

'What is this all about?'

'The Chief Superintendent would like to explain that to you himself.'

Sarah gave the young woman a smile and watched as she turned and walked away without looking back.

For the first few minutes after the time she had set for meeting Annette Fielding, and she had failed to turn up, Sarah was beginning to wonder if she wasn't going to, but then she came hurrying up the stairs from the basement.

'Mr Tyrrell thought that it would be best if we went up to Mr Kershaw's office across the road; his secretary is not there today and we won't be disturbed.'

If Annette Fielding had appeared anxious before, she now looked even more so, with beads of perspiration on her forehead.

'I don't suppose you've been in here before,' Sarah said as she pressed the buzzer on the metal plate by the side of the front door of the block of flats.

'I've met my husband here occasionally at the end of the day's work when he's been dictating notes to Miss Perry.'

'Of course. I should have thought of that.'

Tyrrell was waiting at the door of the flat when they came out of the lift.

'Mrs Fielding?' he said, giving her a smile and holding out his hand. 'My name is Roger Tyrrell and I'm leading the investigation into Mr Kershaw's murder. Why don't we go in here?' he said, making a gesture towards the door with the combination lock on it.

He entered the number on the pad and ushered her into the soundproof room, where she stood, just inside the entrance, her face ashen pale.

'Perhaps you'd take a seat over there,' he said, pointing towards the small settee and then pulled up two chairs and, with Sarah by his side, faced her.

'I won't waste your time by beating about the bush,' he said. 'Just let me say that we know that you used to come up here quite often and what went on between you and Richard Kershaw. We have also seen the still photographs and videos of the sex games you used to play.'

'But—'

'We are also aware that Kershaw went to considerable pains to ensure that you were most carefully disguised by the use of various masks and headdresses, but you failed to take account of the fact that naked bodies, even those with notably unmarked skin, are readily recognized by a police officer experienced in these matters.'

The young woman flushed, stared across at Sarah and made a move to get up from the settee. 'You—'

Tyrrell was already on his feet, and when he looked down at her all the tension went out of her and she slowly sank back.

'That's enough of that. No one asked you to walk around naked by the swimming pool and I suspect that you would never have done so before you started those games with Kershaw. What you did with him must have opened up new possibilities in your sex life. Perhaps you had been a bit shy about your body beforehand and maybe your husband wasn't very adventurous in that direction, but that soon changed, didn't it? Kershaw was something of an obsessional as far as his work was concerned and it appears that that applied to his leisure activities as well. He recorded the dates of your various meetings and of the videos and photographs of what you got up to together. From them, we know how quickly any traces of shyness or reservation on your part disappeared. Now, let me make this very clear; none of what you did with Kershaw was in any way illegal and it only interests us in so far as it might possibly have some bearing on his murder.'

A tear began to trickle down the side of Annette's cheek.

'Does my husband have to know about all this?' she said, her voice almost inaudible. 'It would destroy both him and our marriage if he were to find out what I had been doing with Richard.'

'Not if it has nothing to with his murder. We only found out what was going on between Kershaw and you because we searched this flat and were able to get into his part of it, which, as I am sure you know, has a special security lock on it. Our experts were able to do so without alerting anybody, either Miss Perry, who knows nothing about it at all, or the occupants of the neighbouring flats. We have carried out extensive tests here and the soundproofing is such that nobody in the other part of this flat, the neighbouring ones, the block as a whole, or outside would have heard anything.

'I want you to think very carefully. Did you hint or even boast about what you were doing to anyone, perhaps a girlfriend? Did your behaviour towards your husband change in any way that might have raised his suspicions that you were seeing another man?'

There was a long silence, with Annette Fielding burying her face in her hands, until she finally looked up and wiped the tears away.

'My husband had had no practical experience of sex before we were married and although he must have known about all the variations from his medical studies, he never tried any of them. Richard opened up my mind and body to things which I had never imagined and he did it in such a way that I enjoyed

169

every minute of it. He took his time, never rushed me into anything and in the end I couldn't get enough of it all.

'About six months ago, I started to do some things in bed to my husband that I had learned from Richard, which at first shocked and then excited him and I know, from his reactions since, that we are well on the way to getting that side of things going really well.'

'How did you explain your new know-how in that direction to your husband?'

'I told him that I had been worried about that side of our life together and that I had been to a female marriage guidance counsellor and that she had shown me some videos and had given me a book to read.'

'You were taking a bit of a risk, weren't you?'

'Yes, and you see, Richard had warned me about that on a number of occasions. "Change your routine with your husband," he told me, "and he's bound to wonder." I didn't want to wait; I knew that my relationship with Richard wouldn't last for ever. In many ways I was very fond of John, but I just had to know if I could change his predictable and boring ways in bed. That's why, it must have been about six months ago, I made up the tale of being worried about how ignorant of sex both of us were, how routine and boring it had become, and I told him that I had been seeing the female counsellor I mentioned just now, and what she had said.'

'And you're quite sure that your husband believed you?'

'Oh, yes. I was careful not to try too much to start with and even showed him the book which I had bought at a sex shop.'

'We have seen in the videos that Kershaw had a liking for being beaten; did he ever try to do that sort of thing to you?'

'I was up for it because I saw what an effect it had on him, but all I ever received was a hand spanking a few times. He'd make up a story, such as the time I dressed up in a school uniform and we played out a scene with the headmaster punishing me for stealing a bracelet from one of the other girls. He made it very realistic and I also watched a number of his video tapes and CDs with scenes like that, which really turned me on. I remember asking him if he'd give me a proper caning, but although he said he'd be pleased to do so, it would be too risky and John might see the marks.'

'Any further questions, Sarah?' Tyrrell said.

'Thank you sir. Annette, how realistic do you think the chances are of you now being able to make a success of your marriage?'

'If John were able to get a consultant post well away from here and be his own man, which he was never able to achieve when he was so bound up with Richard, I have no doubt that we would be able to do so.'

'And the sex side?'

'If I'm careful not to be in too much of a hurry, I'm sure we'll be able to make it work really well. I've had my fling and it would be hypocritical to try to pretend that my time with Richard was other than the most exciting of my life, and I can't say I regret it, provided that John doesn't find out about it. He is such a nice man, a bit boring in some ways, but it is now up to me to continue my efforts to make our life together more exciting without diminishing him in any way. I have no

171

doubt that he would make an excellent father if we were to have children, but neither of us is ready for that just yet.

'I am not so naïve as to believe that John would ever forgive me were he to discover what I had been doing with Richard, let alone if he ever got to hear about those recordings and photographs or, even worse, saw them. That would be the finish of our marriage. I am quite certain about that and it wouldn't be the end of it, either. I can see certain sections of the press having a field day if they got hold of them and that might literally kill my father, who is a retired judge. No, I'm not exaggerating; he has heart trouble, is not in the best of health, and it would be too much for him, I just know it would. What is going to happen to all the stuff in here?'

'That will depend on what progress we make in discovering who Kershaw's murderer was,' Tyrrell said. 'If it turns out that your liaison with him had nothing to do with it, then they will be destroyed unless he took any of them away from here, in which case I suppose they might turn up elsewhere.'

The woman's hand suddenly went to her mouth. 'One evening, after we had got dressed and were about to leave, he slipped one of the still photographs that had been processed into the left inside pocket of the jacket of his suit. I remember it vividly because he patted it and said: "As close as possible to my heart! Don't worry, no one could conceivably identify it as being you".'

'Do you remember exactly which photograph that was?'

'Yes. I had been wearing a special headdress – the sort of thing that women wear in the Rio carnivals. It was a favourite of his.'

'We've got his camera and memory cards here and if you are able to give us a rough date of when it was taken, I'm sure we'll be able to find the one in question.'

It took only a matter of minutes before the woman was able to identify it.

'Are you quite sure that this is the one in question?' Tyrrell asked.

'Yes, I remember laughing about it and asked him what that creep of a manservant of his and the starchy Lady Elizabeth would think if they came across it. I didn't put it quite like that, of course.'

'How did he react to that?'

'He just smiled at me and said that he wouldn't care a fig if they did, then he looked at me severely and said that my remark had been very cheeky and that I deserved to be punished.'

'And did he do so?'

'He certainly did. There and then he bent me over the back of the chair I'm sitting in now, lifted up my skirt, pulled down my pants and spanked me harder than he had ever done before. It really hurt, but at the same time turned me on and, despite what we had done earlier that evening, he took me again, holding me down in the position I was already in and didn't wait to undress himself more than the minimum.'

'When did that take place?'

Tyrrell took his diary out of his jacket pocket. 'Can you give me the exact date?'

Annette Fielding ran her finger down the calendar just inside the front page and thought for a minute or two.

173

'Yes,' she said. 'The dinner was definitely on this Thursday and the other was two days before. I remember that because when Richard was taking me into the dining room for dinner after drinks in the drawing room, he put his hand on my bottom and asked in a whisper if I would like a cushion on my chair in there. I was terrified that someone might have overheard.'

'Tell me about the people you met at that dinner.'

'I just couldn't believe either Richard's wife, or his daughter.'

'In what way?'

'Well. Lady Elizabeth looked rather like the picture of Queen Mary I saw in a book about the Royal family, being very stiff and regal and the daughter was obviously ill at ease herself and had very little to say at dinner. I was very surprised when she suggested showing John her father's workshop, and on our way home I asked him about it. All he said was that he had assumed that she must have been concerned about the conversation in the drawing room having become sticky and thought that he might be interested in it.'

'And was he?'

'He certainly was and most impressed by Richard's skill. He also said that his daughter was very nice and, being shy, had obviously been embarrassed by her father's ebullience.' The young woman blushed slightly. 'It was a new word to me and I had to ask John what it meant.'

'Did he tell you?'

'Yes. He said that it described what Kershaw had been like that evening to a T, exuberant and slightly over the top, which was probably due to his having had a drop too much to drink. I can't tell you how relieved I was that John thought that, because I was well aware that Richard's behaviour towards me had been distinctly indiscreet and might have alerted John to what was going on between us. I'm sure that John didn't take it in that way, but that creepy manservant, Parker, certainly did and even had the cheek to warn me about Richard.'

'How did he do that?'

'Not in so many words, of course. He just said, out of John's earshot, as he helped me on with my coat when we were leaving: "Mr Kershaw is a very attractive and clever man and I wouldn't wish you or your husband to be hurt, madam." I realized at once that he must have known about us, but I can't think how he had found out, unless he had managed to read Richard's and my body language that evening.

'Later, I had half a mind to tell Richard what the man had said, but I never did. Funnily, though, that incident acted as a bit of a wake-up call. If Parker had sensed that something was going on between us, then in due course someone else would do so as well. I realize now, too, that the fun and games that the two of us had been enjoying were leading nowhere other than to potential disaster.' The woman looked up and stared at Tyrrell for a moment or two. 'I have been very frank with you, Chief Superintendent, and I realize now that I have only myself to blame for what had happened between Richard and me. I'm not trying to make excuses, but my marriage to John had become boring and would have remained so had he stayed at St Gregory's and been

175

under Richard's thumb. We now have the chance to leave this environment and for John to lighten up and realize that his lack of interest in me sexually has been partly responsible for our marriage being unfulfilling, not only for me, but for him as well. The fact is that he was wedded to his job and not to me. Richard's death has certainly made me take stock of John's and my situation and I have already started to do something about it.

'I have talked to John a good deal since Richard's death and I am sure he understands now just how much he had been neglecting me. John is a good man and I believe that he realizes that he was under Richard's spell, just as I was. His death, appalling though it has been both for his family and for neurosurgery as well, will, I am sure, have liberated both John and me. I can't expect you to understand, but that's the way I see it.'

Tyrrell got to his feet. 'Thank you for being so frank; that's all we need from you for the time being.'

After the young women had gone, Tyrrell watched her through the window as she walked towards the hospital with her umbrella raised.

'What an extraordinary young woman!' he said, turning towards Sarah. 'Initially, I thought that she was not all that bright and was going to play the wronged young wife of Kershaw's first assistant and that she was bored with her marriage and easy meat for the philandering surgeon. It wasn't like that at all, though, was it?'

'I agree. I think she is a very smart operator,' Sarah said. 'She must have known exactly what we had found in this flat, and when I was bringing her here she must have realized that the best line to take was to put a lot of the blame for what happened onto her husband. Maybe that's partly true; it sounds to me as if he is a very worthy but slightly boring individual and a top-class neurosurgeon, but a strong libido and erotic skills seem to have passed him by. By the same token, I wonder if his wife's hopes and expectations of being able to ginger up their sex life are going to be fulfilled.'

'Mark is the one who's seen the most of him,' Tyrrell said, 'so perhaps you'd best ask him what he thinks.'

CHAPTER EIGHT

Lady Elizabeth was still at her son's house when Tyrrell rang her up the following day, and she told him that she was expecting her son and his wife to return the following weekend.

'One small point,' he said, 'and I realize that it may sound an odd thing for me to ask, but do you know how often your husband changed his suits?'

'You'll have to ask Parker about the exact details, because he has always felt it his responsibility to look after all Richard's clothes. Richard never went to the hospital wearing the same suit two days running. Parker used to have a fresh one ready for him each morning and sponge and press the one he had used the previous day. If there was a patch of dirt which he was unable to shift, he would always take it to the dry-cleaners and leave one of the others out for Richard. At least, that's what he always did when I kept a closer eye on the running of the household than I do now, my charity work having become so much more time consuming, but I have no reason to believe that the routine had been changed recently. Thanks to him, Richard was always immaculately turned out when he left for work, with a clean shirt, suitable tie, newly pressed suit and highly polished shoes. I can tell you that it wasn't like that before Parker came to work for us, despite my amateur and well-meaning efforts.'

'Do you use the same dry-cleaner yourself, Lady Elizabeth?'

'Yes, I do and take my clothes there myself, when the need arises, in the car – it is conveniently on the route I take to work and is run by a most charming and helpful Indian man. I've always felt it inappropriate to burden Parker with my clothes on top of everything else he does for us. Apart from that, he has always been very aware of the proprieties and would not countenance doing anything he thought of as being out of place. At one time, I used to have a personal maid of my own, but times change and Parker, the non-resident cleaning lady and the gardener are the only staff we have had for some years.'

The middle-aged Indian who owned and ran the dry cleaning business that the Kershaw household used was slightly built and soft-spoken, with a slight lilt to his voice, but with hardly any accent.

'Of course I know Mr Parker very well,' he said. 'He comes here very frequently with his employer's suits. They're kept very beautifully and, to be honest, they didn't need cleaning as often as they were. I did explain that to do so might well in the end damage the cloth, but he told me that only perfection was good enough for Mr Kershaw and should a suit become worn or damaged in any way, he would always replace it with a new one.' The man smiled. 'Such standards are very rare, these days.'

'Did Mr Kershaw own a lot of suits?'

'I'll just look at my order book – it won't take long; he used our services so frequently that there is a special section for him.' The man pulled out a large book from the shelf beneath the counter and, after looking in the index, found the page. 'Yes, here we are. There were six of them that were cleaned regularly. At this time of year, he used the lighter ones, but he also had heavier ones for use in the winter and then there were two pairs of golfing trousers. In addition, he had a dinner suit, which was always cleaned after every use, and a set of tails.' He ran his finger down the column. 'The tails were last used in December of last year, when Mr Parker told me that Mr Kershaw had attended a dinner in the hall of one of the City livery companies, which was supporting one of his research projects.' The man smiled. 'I can see, sir, that you are surprised that Mr Parker should have discussed such matters with me, a mere dry-cleaning proprietor, but there was a time when I held an academic post in chemistry in Kenya, but things became uncomfortable for me there and I decided to come to this country with my wife and family.'

'Did Mr Parker ever talk to you about his employer?'

'Never, sir. Mr Parker is one of the old school and is a very discreet gentleman. All we ever discussed was the weather and cricket. He is extremely knowledgeable about that and a great admirer of the Indian cricketers and the way they play.'

Tyrrell nodded. 'So am I. Presumably you always check the pockets when you are cleaning mens' suits.

Did you ever find anything in those belonging to Mr Kershaw?'

The man smiled. 'You obviously don't know Mr Parker, sir. He would never overlook details like that.'

'I'm interested in one particular suit. It was most likely brought in on the date I have here.'

'I'll check in my book, sir.' He ran his finger down one of the columns and then looked up. 'Yes, here we are. Mr Parker came in with one on the very date you mentioned.'

'Was there anything unusual about it?'

'Only that Mr Kershaw could only have worn it for a couple of days or so, because it had also been brought in on the Tuesday earlier that week.'

'Did he give any reason for that?'

'There was a small stain on it, near the fly. I remember that because Mr Parker drew my attention to it and I told him that I could easily remove it without having to clean the entire suit. His reply was that Mr Kershaw would not wish to leave the house in clothes that were not immaculate and that he wished to have the whole suit cleaned.'

Tyrrell and his two assistants went to the house in Highgate on the following Tuesday, the day after Lady Elizabeth had returned from her son's house.

'Is all well with your family, Lady Elizabeth?' Tyrrell asked when they were seated in the drawing room.

'Yes, thank you,' she replied. 'Simon and Sophie arrived back here last Friday and I stayed on for a couple of days to allow them to settle in before I returned here. I was afraid that the children might play up as it is the first time that their parents have been away from them for any length of time. It's true that they did for a bit, but soon calmed down.'

'And your son and daughter-in-law had a good time?'

'The break has done them a power of good.' There was a pause and then Lady Elizabeth looked at Tyrrell unblinkingly. 'Now, I don't imagine that you have come here just to chat about my family and welcome me home. Have you made any progress with your enquiry into Richard's death, Chief Superintendent?'

'Yes, to some extent. Firstly, let me assure you that what I have to say is for your ears and your ears only. We have discovered that Kershaw was not the father of your children and, as far as we know, the facts of this matter are known only to you, your elder brother, the present Marquis, and the three of us. As far as we are concerned, we have no reason to believe that that has anything to do with your husband's murder, nor any reason why it should become known to anyone else. The reason we have come today is that we would like to ask Parker one or two more questions and thought it only right to inform you that that is our intention.'

'I can't pretend to understand your reasons for wanting to do so, but I have no objections. However, Parker has no experience of this sort of enquiry. You have already interrogated him at length on his own and I owe it to him to support him and would like to be present on this occasion.'

Tyrrell nodded. 'I have no problem with that.'

'As to the real father of my children,' Lady Elizabeth continued, 'you have no doubt found out about the poor, mentally ill man who was responsible for what

182

happened to me and then took his own life. The continuation or termination of my pregnancy was taken out of my hands by certain members of my family for religious beliefs that I did not and never have shared with them and the consequences of their actions are something I have learned to live with. Of course, I told Richard about it when we discussed the arrangements surrounding our marriage, which had been put to him by my father, and I will always be grateful for his support and friendship over the years. Neither my children nor Parker know anything about what happened at that time and I am quite sure that you are aware of the profound upset that would follow its disclosure now and I very much hope that it will remain confidential, as far as you and your assistants are concerned.'

'I would like to be able to guarantee that none of the information we obtained will get out, because all three of us are well aware of the consequences that would very likely follow,' Tyrrell said, 'but I am unable to do so, as others may make similar enquiries. I believe, though, that that is unlikely to happen, as our informant, the mother of the schizophrenic man who was responsible for what happened to you, is both very old and ill and for various reasons would not like the facts behind that dreadful night to get out, either.'

Lady Elizabeth got slowly to her feet, walked across to the door and pressed the bell push beside it. There was a short pause and then the manservant appeared through the door.

'Ah, Parker.'

'Yes, my lady.'

'The Chief Superintendent would like to ask you a few more questions. Why not draw up that chair and sit down over there?'

Without any change of expression, the man did as asked and perched on the edge of the chair, knees together, and looked in Tyrrell's direction.

'Parker,' the detective said, 'there are a couple of points that I would like clarified. Firstly, the murder weapon was undoubtedly the length of tubular scaffolding that was found by our investigating team propped up against the back wall of the garage only a few feet away from where Mr Kershaw was lying. I was wondering if you noticed it when you went to see why Mr Kershaw was late for tea and whether you had ever seen it before.'

'The answer to both your questions, sir, is no. I was so upset when I saw the state he was in that I very nearly fainted. I knew that I wouldn't be able to do anything to help him on my own and indeed was afraid that if I tried to move him, I might make the situation worse. I hurried back to the house in order to ring for an ambulance. My immediate thought was that Mr Kershaw had fallen down the ladder from his workshop.'

'So you didn't touch him, or anything else?'

'No, sir, I didn't.'

'You didn't consider trying first aid?'

'No, sir. As I have just indicated, I am ignorant of such matters and my immediate thought was to summon professional aid as quickly as possible.'

'How often in the normal course of events did you go into the garage?'

'Only to help Lady Elizabeth to load her car when the need arose.'

'And when was the last time you did that?'

'When she went to look after her grandchildren when her son and daughter-in-law went on holiday recently and, of course yesterday, when she returned.'

'Would you describe exactly how you helped in as much detail as possible, please?'

'She would open the up-and-over door of the garage using her remote control, I would put her case in the boot of her car and, while she was reversing out and closing the door behind her, I would be opening the gates on to the road, so that she could drive out, and shut them again once the car was well clear. After that I would walk back to the house.'

'And when she came back?'

'She would always telephone me from the car when she was nearing the house and I'd open the gate for her in good time and be ready to carry her case back into he house.'

'So you never normally went into the garage by way of the side door?'

'I can only remember having done that once, sir, and that was the dreadful afternoon when Mr Kershaw was late for tea and I found him lying on the floor.'

'And you didn't catch sight of anyone either in the grounds or outside in the road at that time?'

'No, sir.'

Tyrrell nodded. 'Thank you. Now, there is one other matter that I would like to discuss with both you, Parker, and you, Lady Elizabeth, and that is the dinner party that was given for Mr and Mrs Fielding, Mr

Kershaw's first assistant, and his wife a short time ago. Firstly, Lady Elizabeth, the timing of the invitation strikes me as being a little curious and I would value your comments on that. After all, Mr Fielding had been working in that capacity for your husband for a good four years and had never been given hospitality before, so why at that particular time?'

'I sent the invitation at the special request of my husband,' Lady Elizabeth replied. 'He told me that Mr Fielding had been getting restless, was anxious to obtain a consultant post and was beginning to feel that he had been sidelined in terms of promotion. Richard explained that the man was still only in his very early thirties, that there were possibilities for him at St Gregory's and elsewhere, which he had already discussed with him, and that a dinner party here might reassure him that he hadn't been forgotten.'

'I see, thank you. Now, I have already heard accounts of that dinner party from some of those who attended and I would like to hear your views on it first from you, Lady Elizabeth, and then you, Parker. Let me first set the scene, if I may. Mr Fielding clearly gave the impression to both your brother and daughter, Lady Elizabeth, of being anxious, embarrassed even, for most of the evening. Why was that? Did he wonder whether this was a subtle and polite way of Richard Kershaw letting him know that he no longer saw him as being suitable as a future consultant colleague? We know that the man had always been shy and lacked confidence socially, and was that the reason? Certainly, he seemed more at ease after dinner, when your daughter, Mrs Stevens, took him up to the loft above the garage to look at your husband's woodwork. Certainly that was the interpretation she gave me when I spoke to her the other day.

'Now, what about Annette Fielding? From what I've already heard, she seemed to have been as animated as her husband was withdrawn. Was that just because she is that sort of person, or had she had too much to drink? Was Richard Kershaw flirting with her? If he was, she was certainly enjoying it and playing up to it for all she was worth. If that was the case, was she behaving like that because she thought it might help her husband's cause, or was there more to it than that? Were they even having an affair? Mrs Stevens, who was sitting very close to both of them, certainly found their uninhibited behaviour at the dinner table embarrassing.

'Parker, you were in the dining room throughout, apart from short visits to the kitchen. You are an observant and perceptive person and you no doubt detected that there was a certain chemistry between Kershaw and young Mrs Fielding, so much so that you felt the need to give her the most discreet of warnings when you were helping her to put on her coat as she was leaving.

'It didn't work, though, did it, Parker? A few weeks later, you found a photograph of the frontal view of a young woman, who was completely naked apart from an elaborate headdress, in the left inside pocket of the jacket of one of Mr Kershaw's suits. You discovered it, when, as usual, you were making sure that all the pockets were empty, as you always did before hanging the suits up in his wardrobe. That wasn't all, though, was it? You also noticed a stain on the inside of the fly of the trousers, which you decided to have removed at the dry-cleaners. I have had a word with the man who runs that business and he was somewhat surprised at being asked to clean the trousers again, as he had done so only a few days earlier.

'Something or other, perhaps the way Mrs Fielding and Kershaw were talking to each other at dinner, or perhaps he even made an intimate gesture to her when escorting her to the drawing room for coffee, made you reach the conclusion that something was going on between the two of them. No doubt you put two and two together and realized that not only that the young woman in the photograph was very likely to have been Mr Fielding's wife, but also the significance of the stain on his trousers.'

For the first time, Parker looked uneasy, his lips tightly pressed together, and he glanced towards Lady Elizabeth, relaxing slightly as she gave an almost imperceptible nod.

'I would be interested to hear any comment you would like to make about all that,' Tyrrell said.

Lady Elizabeth cleared her throat and before Parker had time to reply, said: 'The Chief Superintendent knows perfectly well, as I do, that you are not obliged to say anything further at this stage, Parker. I will arrange for my solicitor to be present should there be any further questions for you. I am quite sure, too, that what he has just postulated is pure conjecture.'

'It's all right, my Lady,' Parker said. 'A good deal of what the Chief Superintendent said is true: I was concerned about the way Mrs Fielding was responding to Mr Kershaw at the dinner party and even more so when he escorted her to the drawing room for coffee. She and your husband were the last pair to leave after the meal was over and when Mr Kershaw handled her in an extremely intimate fashion when they were walking out of the dining room together, she did not recoil or object, merely smiling and saying something very quietly to him. What was I to do? Say nothing at all, mention the incident to Lady Elizabeth or what I decided on, which was to make a very brief comment to the young woman as I was helping her on with her coat at the end of the evening.'

'What exactly did you say?'

'I am unable to remember the exact words, sir, but something to the effect that Mr Kershaw was a very attractive man and that I wouldn't want her to be hurt in any way.'

'I see. Now, one last matter: I heard this morning that some specimens of DNA have been found on the murder weapon other than that of Mr Kershaw. I am arranging for a specimen to be taken from Mr Stacey, who remembers bringing the piece of scaffolding in from the undergrowth in the garden and although you, Lady Elizabeth and you, Parker, appear never to have handled it, I would also like specimens to be taken from both of you. As you may already know, the procedure is quite painless and does not involve the use of needles.'

'Your explanation seems somewhat tortuous, Chief Superintendent, but I have no objection and I don't suppose you have either, Parker.'

'No, my lady, I don't.'

'What did you make of all that?' Tyrrell said when they

were back at the Yard. 'Sarah, perhaps you'd go first. You were the one to see Annette Fielding both on your own as well as at the flat.'

'Yes,' Sarah said. 'Parker's account seems to me to be quite convincing and I can't see him being capable of or even wanting to harm Kershaw in any way physically. It's true that he doesn't appear to have known about Lady Elizabeth's celibate marriage and I suppose that even a man of his age and slight physique might have had the strength to shatter Kershaw's skull, but the actions he described after finding his employer dead strike me as being both sensible and reasonable. Also, his warning to Annette Fielding and the actions he took over the photograph and the stained trousers seem purely to have been directed towards protecting Lady Elizabeth from what her husband had been up to rather than anything else. As to the murderer, it seems to me that the man, whose wife died following surgery by Kershaw, or John Fielding are more likely candidates.

'The former seems to have been on a short fuse and to have blamed Kershaw for what happened, and if Fielding found out about his wife's behaviour and infidelity, he must also be in the frame. Mark has seen both of them at length and I would be very interested to hear what he thinks about them.'

'Mark?' Tyrrell said.

'I agree with what Sarah said about Parker, and as for Fielding, all I can say about him is that he struck me as being a very conscientious man, verging on the pathologically obsessional. Everything he told me was reasonable, but if he had indeed found out what his wife had been up to, I suppose he might have reacted violently. However, nothing I have heard about him leads me to suppose that he has ever been impulsive or ill tempered, rather the reverse, in fact. Certainly, according to Morley's account, he reacted both calmly and patiently to the man's outburst over his wife's death after her operation.'

'Right. I agree that the person who murdered Kershaw is most likely to have been someone who knew that the man would very likely be in his workshop on a Sunday afternoon, and that suggests either a member of the family or Fielding. If we're agreed about that, what's next? Sarah?'

'I'd like to have another talk to Rebecca Cochrane. I got the strong impression that she was holding something back.'

'Mark?'

'As you've pointed out, sir, both Fielding, if he knew about her infidelity, and Morley, on account of his blaming Kershaw for his wife's death, must still be suspects. Either of them would have had the time to have gone to Highgate and back on that Sunday by car, taxi or underground, and I suggest that I look further into that, although I'm not optimistic about the outcome.'

'That all makes good sense to me. I'll give you both a couple of days to organize all that and then we'll meet again. Tredgold wouldn't tell me about the DNA details when he rang this morning and I will arrange for us to see him again directly he's got answers from the specimens from Lady Elizabeth and Parker. Later on, we may well need to get Fielding and Morley tested as well.'

*

Sarah Prescott decided to call on Rebecca Cochrane that evening without prior warning and it had the desired effect. The woman opened the door on the chain and the look on her face betrayed her anxiety.

'I've had a very long day,' she said, 'and I've had about as much as I can take. Can't what you want to discuss wait until tomorrow?'

'No, it can't,' Sarah said firmly, 'it's far too important for that.'

Rebecca opened the door and backed away as the detective moved past her. 'Let's go into the sitting room, shall we?'

With obvious reluctance, the woman led the way, made a gesture towards one of the easy chairs and then perched on the edge of her own.

'I'm not going to put up with either prevarication or half-truths. Did you or did you not tell John Fielding what his wife was up to with Richard Kershaw?'

All the colour had left the woman's cheeks and she dropped her head.

'I'm waiting.'

'I felt I had to do it,' she said, after a long pause, her voice almost inaudible.

'You'd better explain.'

Rebecca Cochrane and John Fielding had arrived at St Gregory's Hospital Medical School on the same day. There were many similarities between the two of them; both were extremely bright academically and hard working, they were both uncertain with the opposite gender, having been to single-sex, private boarding schools and they didn't fit in at all with the others, being painfully inept socially. Rebecca compensated for that by being forthright to the point of rudeness and John, being very shy, withdrew into himself.

Rebecca never looked upon herself as being gay, at least not in the physical sense of that term. It was true that she preferred the company of women to that of men, but even that wasn't always the case. She was no more able to tolerate obsession with clothes and beauty treatments than he could with sport and football. As for heavy drinking, she despised it, whether in men or women. Inevitably, with those attitudes, there were snide remarks made about her sexuality, or lack of it, but people never dared to make them to her face. As for Fielding, at least no one suggested that he was a homosexual but, like Rebecca, he stood out from the others and dealt with that by working obsessively. Such leisure activities as he had were almost exclusively solitary. He had been a talented chess player at school, but was unable to find a kindred spirit at St Gregory's and spent hours studying famous games from the past and playing against his Kasparov electronic machine at the top level of difficulty.

Clever though she was, Rebecca lacked spatial skills, which made anatomy more difficult for her than the other disciplines. One day, she was in the library trying to make sense of the course of the visual pathways without any success and, after half an hour, she shook her head in pure frustration and slammed shut her copy of *Gray's Anatomy*.

'Having problems?'

Rebecca looked up, an acid response on the tip of her tongue, but when she saw who it was she promptly stifled it and let out a sigh.

'I know it must sound pathetic, but I just can't get a grip of the visual pathways.'

'Perhaps I'll be able to help you.'

Had it been anyone else, she might have given him the brush-off, but she knew John Fielding just well enough to know that he meant exactly what he had said, no more and no less, and wasn't trying anything on. That was the start of it. He was a gifted board artist and was able to pick out the anatomical pathways and their relationship to other structures in a way that simplified what at first sight had seemed to her to be complicated and impenetrable.

It would never have worked had their relationship been one-sided, but it wasn't, his weakness being lack of confidence in dealing with people and, in particular, patients. The course they were following was fully integrated in that they had contact with patients right from the beginning and, for Fielding, that was something of a nightmare. He was only too well aware that he was diffident and awkward with his peers and the thought of having to relate to complete strangers was even worse. Rebecca, though, despite being acerbic and unpopular with her fellow students, men and women, had an instinctive skill in getting ill people to talk to her.

'I just don't know how to communicate with patients, let alone put them at their ease,' Fielding said to her one day when they were having lunch with one another in the canteen. 'They're obviously as embarrassed as I

am and the result is that we both become tongue-tied.
I've been told to take a history from an elderly man and
I've no idea at all how to set about it.'

'All you need to do,' Rebecca said, 'is to make human
contact with them before you get on to the medical
details. Look, I've also been told to take a history from
someone on one of the medical wards and all I know is
that she's expecting me and her name and age. Why not
come along with me and I'll try to show you what I
mean?'

As they approached, Fielding knew immediately that
he wouldn't have had the slightest idea how to begin
had the elderly woman been his responsibility. She
appeared to be in her early seventies and let out a sigh
as they approached, putting her knitting down beside
her.

'Hello,' Rebecca said, 'I'm Rebecca and this is John. I
hope that someone has told you that we are students,
and it's very good of you to talk to us and we're sorry to
interrupt your knitting.'

'That's all right, dear, my old eyes need a rest.'

'I very much regret never having learned how to knit;
apart from being so useful, it must be very relaxing.'

The elderly woman smiled. 'Everything's such a rush
these days, isn't it? Now, what is it you want to know?'

Fifteen minutes later, they left the woman's bedside
after Rebecca had thanked her for her help and said
goodbye.

'And so you see, John, it's not that difficult. That old
lady is obviously an old hand with students, which is no
doubt why she was selected for me in order to let me in
gently. I can't pretend that I worked out the best way to

handle patients entirely on my own. My father is a psychiatrist at the Henshaw Hospital and he has been a great help to me. He hasn't confused me with elaborate theories and just said that although it was important to learn from one's teachers, I shouldn't try to copy them, just use my strengths and guard against my weaknesses. He got me to take histories from him, playing the part of different patients, some of whom were easy to deal with, like that old lady we've just seen, and others, who were rude and aggressive, and some who tried to flirt with me. He also discussed with me the best way to break news of serious illness or the need for an operation and all along pointed out that no two patients are alike in their reactions to doctors and the news one has to break to them. "Don't take rudeness or bloody mindedness to heart," he said. "Dealing with that is part of the territory, but don't go away thinking that that is the rule, because it isn't. The great majority of patients realize that one is there to help and do appreciate one's efforts, even though they don't always say so."

'He also told me to watch and listen to the medical staff and analyze those who do it well and those who do it badly and to learn from both. Finally, he told me to be aware of my own shortcomings and work out ways to overcome them.'

It didn't surprise Rebecca in the least that John should have taken what she had said to heart, but what did was his success in applying it. It took quite a long time, but he worked at it and discovered that it was a great deal easier to relate to his patients than to his peers. It was that skill that made him such a success as a surgeon. He certainly didn't have quite the same manual dexterity as Kershaw, but he more than made up for that with his skill in handling patients and their relatives. True, he did remain a little shy and diffident, but even that added to the calming effect he had on anxious and, in particular, angry ones.

After she had been appointed as a consultant herself, Rebecca had witnessed Fielding at work on a number of occasions with those of her own patients who had developed problems requiring neurosurgical intervention. He had a gift for using simple language, but he never talked down to patients, nor falsely diminished the risks. What he had to say was the truth as he saw it, and people believed him.

Socially, he remained painfully shy, but he always had plenty to say to Rebecca, perhaps, she thought, because they knew each other so well and he didn't feel threatened by her. He must, she thought, have noticed that she never seemed to go out with any of the students, male or female, but sexuality in any shape or form was something that they never discussed and she kept her fantasies about women very carefully hidden and had disciplined herself never to have a physical relationship with anyone. She had no idea if John had any impulses in that direction, or any other for that matter. As far as she was concerned, he was just a friend, who shared her interests in music, the theatre, films and, above all, medicine.

It came as a complete surprise when he told her that he had met a young woman at a party on the Isle of Wight, where his parents had retired. It was obvious to Rebecca that he was completely besotted by her. She was so pretty, he said, such fun and he could talk to her about anything.

Rebecca met the young woman for the first time when John's parents invited her to spend a weekend on the island. It was at a party and she was at a complete loss to comprehend the attraction between the two of them. Despite being in her early twenties and having obtained 'A' levels, she looked and behaved as if she was still in her late teens. It was some six months later, by which time he and Rebecca had been senior registrars for two years, that he told her that he was getting engaged to Annette and that they were planning to get married that summer.

It seemed to Rebecca that when Annette and her mother came up to London to see about her wedding dress, the young woman hadn't changed at all and in no way did she see her coping as a newly married woman, let alone one who would be living a long way away from her family, with a husband who had an extremely demanding job.

Rebecca was proved right. After only three months of married life, she saw that Annette was bored out of her mind and determined to help her in any way she could. She invited her to lunch in the hospital canteen and then suggested that she might like to go swimming with her regularly each week in the nurses' pool. John and Annette had been married for about eighteen months when Rebecca told Annette that she ought to get a job and, after long discussions between the three of them, she agreed to apply for training as a technician in the hospital department of clinical electrophysiology. After all, Rebecca said to her, with 'A' levels in physics and chemistry, she had the right grounding for it and it was about time that she stopped pretending that she was an airhead. John was very keen on the idea and eventually Annette did agree, albeit with great reluctance. Rebecca, by this time, was a consultant and with her and John's support, Annette obtained the appointment and started as a trainee.

It was a few months later that Rebecca began to notice a change in the young woman's behaviour. She began to use coarse and occasionally obscene language, went into the open shower at the back of the swimming pool with nothing on, and when she came out, just stood there, chatting and making no attempt to cover herself up with her towel. Not only did Rebecca find that embarrassing, but there was a real risk of one of the nurses, or even the formidable sister tutor, coming in, which at best would have meant the end of their swims and, at worst, an unholy row with the authorities.

Rebecca knew with absolute certainty that John would be just as concerned by such behaviour as she was, and disclosure of it might even have an adverse effect on his future prospects of getting a consultant post. Might it also mean that Annette was seeing someone else? It seemed quite possible. Rebecca did have a tentative word with the young woman about it, but that was met with scorn. 'What are you on about?' she said, 'we're living in the twenty-first century, aren't we; at least I am. If the men can walk about with nothing on when they are alone together or in a group, why shouldn't we?'

Although she hated herself for it, late one afternoon, Rebecca followed Annette when she knew that John was involved in a lengthy operation on a patient's spine. She knew she was right when, on leaving the hospital, her friend took a circuitous route to the back of the block of flats where Kershaw had his office and was let in through the rear entrance. He had to be the one whom Annette was meeting and Rebecca was determined to prove it. She couldn't believe that the young woman would risk departing by the front entrance at that time of day and, sure enough, an hour later, she saw her come out at the back and make off in the direction of the underground station.

Any doubts she might have had were stilled when, forty-five minutes later, John Fielding smiled at her and gave her a wave as he passed through the front hall of the hospital where she was sitting. Walking as far as the front doors, she saw him cross the square and go in through the main entrance to the block of flats. Ten minutes later, he came out again with Kershaw at his side and after a few words the two men walked towards their respective cars.

'So it was then that you decided to tell John about what was going on?' Sarah said.

'Yes, I did, and although it pains me to say this, I believe that Kershaw's death is the one thing that might save their marriage and I am sure that their best move would be for them to leave London.'

'How did Fielding react to what you said?'

'John has never been one to show his emotions or say very much. After I had finished, he just said: "Are you quite sure about all this?" '

'I explained how he must have noticed how much

Annette had changed in the preceding few months, about her behaviour at the swimming pool and how I had seen her go in through the back entrance of the block of flats and come out the same way an hour later while he had been operating late that afternoon.'

'How did he take that?'

'I remember that all he did was to nod and thank me and then he walked away without saying another word.'

'How long was that before Kershaw's murder?'

'It must have been about ten days.'

'What about the behaviour of the two of them since?'

'Annette has avoided me completely since that day when you were with us at the pool. I think that she put on that special exhibition in order to embarrass me and end our friendship. Perhaps, too, she was afraid that I had noticed something suspicious about her behaviour and that I might find out about her relationship with Kershaw.'

'Do you think that John Fielding had it in him to kill someone if the provocation was sufficient?'

'The very idea is ridiculous. I have known John for more than ten years and I'm willing to bet that he has never had a violent or aggressive thought in his mind.'

'If you are right about that, who do you think might have been driven to murder Kershaw?'

'I can't believe that Annette was the only woman whom Kershaw entertained in his flat and perhaps another wronged husband was responsible. He also had many enemies on the staff. Perhaps even someone in his family found out what he was up to and decided to kill him.'

*

It took Sinclair less than half an hour to discover that
Fielding had arrived at the hospital soon after two
o'clock on the Sunday afternoon that Kershaw was
murdered. Reg Banks, one of the porters who liked to
work on Sundays, lived only a quarter of a mile away
and after Benson, the head porter, had telephoned him,
he came round and met the detective in the front hall.

'Yes, sir,' he said. 'I'm quite sure that Mr Fielding was
here as usual that afternoon. I remember that it was
sunny and I was standing on the steps outside the main
entrance when he drove up and parked in his allocated
space over there. He has a black VW Golf, and after he
had got out he walked through the entrance to the block
of flats over there where Mr Kershaw had his office.'

'Did he seem his usual self?'

'Indeed he did, sir. He gave me a wave and a smile as
always. A very nice gentleman is Mr Fielding, sir, very
friendly, and just before he left, it must have been about
five-thirty, he came across and we had a brief chat
about the cricket.'

'And did you see him in between those times?'

'No, sir, I didn't.'

Although he knew that it would almost certainly be a
waste of time, Sinclair started his stopwatch at the rear
entrance to the block, walked steadily to the nearest
underground station and took the Northern Line to
Highgate and from there finished the journey to
Kershaw's house on foot. It took him just under forty-
five minutes and rather more to get back. It would
certainly have been possible for Fielding to have done
the double journey and murdered Kershaw that
afternoon, but there wouldn't have been all that much

time to spare and it seemed highly unlikely that he would have been able to get back and be chatting to the porter, seemingly his usual self, by five-thirty.

Before going back home, though, armed with the registration number of Morley's Alfa Romeo, he spent half an hour walking around the area in Fulham where the man's flat was situated. It was immediately obvious that it was going to be a waste of time. There were literally hundreds of cars in the immediate locality, parked head to tail in all the side roads and the chances of finding anyone who had noticed the Alfa leaving that afternoon, would, he reckoned, be negligible. The man would also, unlike Fielding, have had the whole afternoon to have made the journey to Highgate by taxi or public transport. Finally, although he was well aware that it would almost certainly be a waste of time, when he got to the Yard the following morning, he detailed one of the WPCs to check the drivers in the taxi ranks in the area.

CHAPTER NINE

The three detectives met Eric Tredgold in his office three days later.

'As ever, my dear Tyrrell, you don't disappoint me,' the forensic pathologist said, once his long-suffering secretary had brought in the coffee and biscuits. 'That mundane object, the length of tubular scaffolding, has yielded some evidence that you might find of interest. In addition, apart from the victim's blood, there were two other specimens of DNA on it. One of them matched that which you obtained from the gardener, but, although the other was not on the data base, it definitely came from a woman.' The man saw Tyrrell's raised eyebrows and gave a chuckle. 'Yes, a woman, and I take it from your expression that you are surprised. Perhaps you have good reason to be so; you see, the woman is clearly not related to Kershaw, but most certainly is to his wife, Lady Elizabeth, and closely at that.'

'Ah,' Tyrrell said. 'We know that Alison Stevens, who is Lady Elizabeth's natural daughter, went through the garage on the evening that a dinner party was given for Kershaw's first assistant, one John Fielding, and his

204

wife. It's possible that she just touched the murder weapon, which was resting against the back wall of the garage as she went to show Fielding Kershaw's workshop and his carvings up in the loft, but that strikes me as highly unlikely as she was dressed for dinner and had no reason to do so. In any case, clearly the time has come to question her again.'

'I take it, from the way you put it, that Kershaw was not her father.'

'Indeed, he was not. Lady Elizabeth was raped by a schizophrenic, who had absconded from a mental hospital during the night after a party given to celebrate her eighteenth birthday, and twins, a boy and a girl, were the result. I won't go into the details, and I'm sure that you will understand that this information is strictly confidential, but we discovered that her marriage to Kershaw was one of convenience and he was not the father of the children. Lady Elizabeth decided never to tell them, which may have been the tragic error that led to his death.'

'I get the general drift,' Tredgold said, 'but why should this woman, Alison Stevens, have decided to kill him if she was unaware that he was not her father?'

'I have some ideas about that and I believe we now have enough evidence to interview her under caution, get a DNA sample from her and, if there is a match with the specimen you tested from the scaffolding tube, then we will probably be able to charge her.'

The interview with Alison Stevens was conducted by Tyrrell at Scotland Yard in the presence of his two assistants, her mother, Lady Elizabeth Kershaw, and

205

her solicitor. After formally introducing himself, Sinclair and Prescott, and Alison Stevens had confirmed her name and address, Tyrell said:

'We have reason to believe that you hit Richard Kershaw on the back of his head with the length of tubular scaffolding, which had been resting against the back wall of his garage. He had been working up in the loft above at his hobby of making, dolls' house furniture and appears to have come backwards down the wooden staircase for his tea break on Sunday, just over two weeks ago. It appears that he had just reached the floor when the blow which killed him was delivered. On the weapon was his blood, from which his DNA was extracted. There were two other samples on it, that of the gardener, who had found the tube in the undergrowth and brought it into the garage with a view to disposing of it, and the other matches yours, Mrs Stevens.

'I believe that you wish to make a statement with regard to these matters and know that it will be recorded and may be used in evidence.'

Alison looked straight at the detective and said, 'Yes, I do.'

With occasional glances at her mother and down at her notes, Alison Stevens spoke in a soft, but clear voice.

'My twin brother, Simon, and I must have been a sad disappointment to Richard Kershaw as neither of us showed his artistic talents, nor his remarkable hand-eye coordination that made him such a brilliant games' player and surgeon. That particularly applied to me; I hated ball games of any description, whereas Simon, although not good at them, at least tried his best and

206

obviously got enjoyment out of them.

'From what I gathered from my mother, I was very like her as a child, with my head always in a book, very shy and, quite clearly, not a lot of fun. Whereas I was a hard worker at school and obsessional with regard to my studies, you will have heard that Richard was the very reverse of that, being gregarious and both physically and intellectually like quicksilver. I can't claim that he ignored me, and his discussing books and listening to my opinions on all sorts of subjects are the happiest memories I have of him, nor did he spend more time with my less intense and much more friendly brother.

'I was not unhappy during my early childhood. I got on well at school and the fact that I had virtually no friends did not worry me or my mother at all. As she explained to me, and perhaps even Richard as well, lots of people, including herself, were like that, too, and the important thing was to accept the sort of person one was and be content with the deal one had been given.

'The first real cloud on the horizon, and it was a large black one, appeared when I was twelve and physically young for my age. The four of us went to St Moritz one Easter for a skiing holiday. Needless to say, Richard was a real expert, whereas my mother confined herself to some elegant and unadventurous skating. On the other hand, Simon, as he always did with everything else, though not being naturally good at it, entered into it with the greatest enthusiasm and made good progress. I hated it. I couldn't see the point, I kept falling over and the cold made it doubly unpleasant for me. After a few days, I couldn't face it any more and pretended to have a really bad stomach ache. My mother was convinced that I had acute appendicitis and was all for bringing in the hotel doctor.

'Richard would have none of that and said that he would take a look at me himself. While he did so, my mother turned her head away and kept her eyes focused on the view through the window. Richard inspected my tongue, took my temperature and then told me to lie on my back and pull my nightdress up to my chest. He adjusted the sheet so that it covered the lower part of my body, then pressed very gently all over my abdomen with his warm and beautifully shaped and manicured hands.

"Nothing to worry about," he said when he had finished. "A hot water bottle and nothing to eat or drink for the time being will do the trick. I'll come and take another look at you after we've had our lunch."

'My mother asked me if I'd like her to sit and read to me, but I persuaded her not to, saying that I would just have a sleep. In fact, all that was wrong with me was hunger, and the bar of chocolate that was in the chest of drawers was some help.

'Richard came back soon after lunch, pulled up a chair by the side of the bed and said: "You know and I know that there's nothing wrong with you at all, Alison. If you don't like skiing and want to stop, why not say so instead of pretending to be unwell? What you did can be dangerous – you might even have had an unnecessary operation on your appendix. Telling lies like that is a stupid thing to do and I am going to do something that, if you are ever tempted to do such a thing again, will, I hope, act as a reminder. When I have finished, you will have a bath, get dressed and then we'll all have a proper tea at that restaurant you like so much. I see no reason why I should tell your mother what you did or about the consequences that followed."

'He remained sitting on his chair, told me to get out of bed, then pulled me over his knees and lifted my nightdress up to my waist. He then spanked me really hard with his hand. I was determined not to give him the satisfaction of crying, calling out or begging him to stop, and when he had finished, I got to my feet and, without looking in his direction, went into the bathroom.

'It was not much later, when I had attended a sex talk with the female doctor at my school, who spoke to us individually, and had read some books on the subject, that I realized the significance of both the extraordinary feeling I had had inside me as I looked at my bright-red bottom in the mirror in the bathroom in that hotel and the swelling in Richard's trousers which I had felt beneath me.

'Richard behaved perfectly normally in the café later that afternoon and it was obvious that my mother knew nothing about the whole thing, being just relieved that I had recovered so quickly. I realized later that Richard had been quite right to teach me a sharp lesson, but it was not long after that that other incidents began to occur when my mother and brother were out of the way. I was terrified at the thought that he might punish me even more severely if I tried to resist what he was doing and, in any case, he never hurt me and, to my shame, I even experienced pleasure at what was happening to me. In a way, ignorant though I was, I sensed that what

209

he was doing was wrong, but I remembered only too vividly what had happened at the ski resort and so I did nothing. In any case, I have to admit that I enjoyed a lot of what he did to me. There was no question of my telling my mother, either. How could I, when she was so remote and I didn't really understand what was going on myself?

'And so I said nothing to her or anyone else about it. I didn't have access to the appropriate books, but I did to the Internet and it was only then that I fully understood the full extent and significance of what he was doing to me and I started to take steps to protect myself from him. I always locked the doors both to the bathroom and my bedroom whenever I was in them alone, I refused to go to the local swimming pool with him without my mother being present as well and, armed with a recommendation from the head teacher of my local day school, I persuaded my mother to send me away to boarding school when I was thirteen.

'Before today, I have never spoken to my mother about it or anything to do with it, but surely she must have guessed that something had happened between Richard and me. Anyway, by then, Richard had backed off completely and I suppose one could say that there was some sort of truce and understanding between us. That was never voiced, but after I had gone to the boarding school, he never so much as spoke to me unless my mother was present or Uncle James was there, when he joined in with the conversation in his usual urbane manner. On those occasions, I made a point of being polite, telling them how I was getting on at school and my hopes of getting a university place.

'Deep down inside me, though, I remained deeply resentful of what he had done to me and partly because of that and partly because I didn't want my fellow students at university to know that I had connections with the aristocracy, when I was eighteen and between leaving school and going to Bristol, I changed my name by deed poll, and soon after decided to pretend that I had got married and made up a husband so as to avoid the attentions of the male students.

'I made no attempt to explain what was going on to my mother, brother, or my favourite uncle, James. I did see them from time to time, but the subject of Richard and the reason for my having become so remote from my family were never broached. After I had obtained my degree and become articled to a firm of solicitors, I let it be known that I had recently been divorced. Obviously, as Chief Superintendent Tyrrell was so easily able to find out all about this merely by consulting records, both my mother and Richard could have done so just as simply. Perhaps she thought that as I had managed to forge a satisfactory life for myself she didn't wish to interfere and, not surprisingly, Richard wanted nothing to do with me in any way other than the absolute minimum.

'I know how much it will hurt my mother to hear all this, but it was only too obvious to me as an adult that, in some senses, like me, she lived in a half-world and was only able to relate to people at one remove. For her, it was with those she met in her charitable and community work and at least I knew that she was comfortable with Parker as an ever reliable and non-judgemental presence. I never have been able to understand how or why, on the surface, she seemed to get on so well with Richard and tolerated his obvious indiscretions. There's no denying that they seemed genuinely fond of one another, but never once did I see them share an intimate gesture and I just could not imagine them ever having had a physical relationship of any sort.

'Why, then, when I had made a separate life for myself and was as happy with it as my personality allowed, did I agree to go to my mother's dinner party? That was really my Uncle James's responsibility. He explained to me that my mother was concerned about Richard's first assistant, John Fielding, whom she had met at the hospital at a memorial service for one of Richard's former mentors. She had heard that he was being exploited by Richard and that his young wife was being neglected and was unhappy. As result, she asked her brother, James, for his advice as she was thinking about giving a dinner party for the two of them and wondered if it would be a good idea to invite him and me as well. Uncle James didn't know the truth about Richard Kershaw and me, but our estrangement was only too obvious and perhaps he thought that it might be an opportunity to mend a few fences between the two of us, as well as giving himself an opportunity to drop a few hints in Richard's direction about the man's wife, should it be obvious that he was flirting with her. I was not at all keen on the idea as far as I was concerned and hesitated before accepting, but James was his usual cheerful and persuasive self and so I did agree to go. Some guilt about my distant relationship with my mother also played a part.

'Anyway, I have spent a great deal of my time studying men and women in unhappy marital situations; by no means all of them have ended up in the divorce courts and I like to think that my attempts at mediation have helped in quite a number. James was not suggesting that I tackled my father about it, but that I might be able to discuss the situation with my mother, who had raised the issue in the first place and either reassure her or give her the benefit of my advice.

'You won't be surprised to hear that I summed up the situation between John and Annette Fielding within minutes of talking to him. He was a thoroughly nice young man, serious, overconscientious, dedicated to his work and, without doubt, being exploited by Richard. Why else had he been slaving away for so long without getting promotion?

'As I was sitting next to Richard, with Annette on his other side, it was immediately obvious to me, and I would have thought to everyone else who was there as well, that they were having an affaire. It was the way that they were talking to each other and their body language, with Richard's eyes fixed on her décolletage and her simpering and flaunting her very considerable assets.

'I was really angry at the way Richard was behaving and it was just as well that he ignored me more or less completely, hardly even glancing in my direction. I might well have made some acid comment there and then and upset my mother, who has always been one for the proprieties. As a result, I took the opportunity to talk to John Fielding, who was on my left. I had seen that scenario so often in my work. The man was

intense, serious and worthy and to many must have
seemed rather boring, totally dedicated to his
profession and with something of a hero complex with
regard to Richard. As for sex, I sensed that she had
probably been introduced to all the variations by
Richard and that she couldn't get enough of it, whereas
for him, he was quite likely to be a once a week man, if
she was lucky, and that with the lights out.'

'I became increasingly more angry as the evening
progressed and that is why I offered to show Fielding
Richard's workshop. Spending even such a short time
with him, I could see that he was clearly not made of
stone and that he must have known perfectly well what
was going on, but had no idea what to do about it. It was
also obvious to me what a thoroughly nice man he was.
As for Annette, seeing the way that she had behaved
throughout the evening and that it continued as she
was leaving, I knew that the two of them were never
going to settle down together. Having come across
similar situations so often in my work, I could see
nothing but misery ahead for the wretched Fielding.

'My anger with Richard over his treatment of my
mother, his bullying of Fielding, his exploitation of the
man's silly wife and what he had done to me all those
years ago was such that I knew there and then that I
was going to have to do something about it. I swear I
just went to his house in Highgate that afternoon, when
I knew that my mother would be away looking after her
grandchildren, merely with the intention of telling him
face to face exactly what I thought of him in the vain
hope that it might make some difference to the lives of
those two young people. It was not to be: as I watched

him come down the ladder from his workshop in the
garage, whistling and obviously quite happy with his
life, I suddenly lost control, snatched up that pole and
hit him as hard as I could.

'What do I feel now? I know that to say "if only" to
myself is absurd, but that is what I have done. If only
my mother had been less remote, had discussed sex and
life in general with me before my adolescence, I might
have been able to deal with Richard's behaviour
towards me. You see, it wasn't that he was ever at all
brutal, or ever hurt me. He was far more subtle than
that and to my shame I have to admit that I actively
enjoyed a lot of it, which later added to my shame and
guilt. It would be unfair to blame my mother for what
happened, but I couldn't help thinking that if she had
been a more motherly and observant person, perhaps
she would have realized the full extent of what Richard
did to me as a child and intervened in some way or
other. While I have no intention of revealing the exact
details of how far he went with me, let me just say that
it shaped my life and left me bitter and twisted inside.
I knew, too, that in their own way, my mother and
Richard got on well together, which in some ways has
made it that much worse for me, almost as if she had
been colluding with what happened. There was never
any tension between them, let alone arguments or rows,
and I am only too well aware what a loss to
neurosurgery was Richard's death.

'Will there be any benefits at all from the awful thing
that I did? That certainly won't be true for my mother,
my brother and his family, nor my uncle James, but
what about the Fieldings? Will he now be able to equal

215

Richard's achievements in the field of neurosurgery, will his wife grow up and their marriage succeed? Will my mother explain what led to this to my twin brother, my uncle James and also Parker, who has always been there for her. I hope so, and perhaps in time they might even forgive me.

'It is my intention to plead guilty in court and not to claim mitigating factors in order to protect my mother and other members of my family from the public airing of all these secrets.'

CHAPTER TEN

It was a few months later that Tyrrell and his two assistants attended the trial of Alison Stevens for the murder of Richard Kershaw, which was heard without a jury as she had admitted guilt and had expressed a wish that no extenuating circumstances should be aired in court. However, Lady Elizabeth would have none of it, and one of the top barristers represented her and made a plea for a verdict of manslaughter. He went on to describe the abuse she had suffered at the hands of Richard Kershaw as a child and how she had never got over it. She had also discovered later that he was being unfaithful to her mother and had gone to the house that Sunday afternoon while her mother was away looking after her grandchildren, meaning to confront him verbally. However, when she saw him descending the ladder from his workshop in the garage, whistling and obviously happy, something snapped inside her. She caught sight of the tube of scaffolding, snatched it up and, without premeditation, hit him over the head with it.

Lady Elizabeth had very clearly decided to be

selective in what she told the barrister. There was no mention of the circumstances of her own rape at the age of eighteen by the schizophrenic patient who had absconded from hospital, or the resulting pregnancy with twins and the religious reasons why the idea of a termination had not even been contemplated, or her hurried marriage to Richard Kershaw. The barrister dwelt at length on the physical and sexual abuse that Alison had suffered since the age of twelve at Kershaw's hands and the steps she had taken to distance herself from him. He described how she had first persuaded her mother to send her to a boarding school and how, later, she had achieved a place at university, had changed her name by deed poll and pretended to have been married and divorced. As a result, she had achieved complete independence from Kershaw and had forged a successful career as a solicitor.

Her mother had known about none of this and accepted that Alison, who had always been shy and withdrawn, had decided that she wanted to live her life independently and in her own way. The two of them continued to meet and had a comfortable, if not close, relationship with one another.

The incident that had sparked the tragedy of Kershaw's death, the barrister said, was the dinner party that the Kershaws gave for one of his colleagues and his young wife. Lady Elizabeth had persuaded Alison to join the party, feeling that it was high time that there was a rapprochement between father and daughter, who, for reasons she had never understood, had always failed to get on with each other. He went on to reiterate the circumstances that Alison had described in her statement that led to her hitting Kershaw.

In his closing speech, he made a case for a verdict of manslaughter. There had been no premeditation, no intent to kill when the accused had set out to confront her father, but when she saw him descending the ladder from his workshop, whistling and in an obviously happy mood, her control snapped. The memory of all those years of abuse came flooding back and she picked up the length of scaffolding, which she saw resting against the wall of the garage, and hit him over the head with it.

The judge went into a lengthy explanation of the difference between murder and manslaughter and the lack of malice in the latter. Provocation in manslaughter had to be shown to be recent and reasonable, he pointed out and did not apply if express malice is proved. There had been mitigating factors in the case under consideration and there had been a lack of premeditation and any intention had been to cause serious bodily harm rather than to kill, but nevertheless there had not been sufficient in the way of mitigating factors to accept such a verdict.

A verdict of murder was brought in and when it came to determining the term of imprisonment, there was further detailed argument. A starting point of fifteen years in prison was determined but, in view of the mitigating factors and the fact that the accused had pleaded guilty at the earliest possible opportunity, a minimum term of five years in prison was decided upon before consideration would be given by the parole board as to whether release was appropriate.

With the accused having pleaded guilty, the family

refusing to respond to requests for interviews and the hospital authorities merely issuing anodyne statements, media interest in the case soon evaporated.

It was nearly six weeks later that Tyrrell arranged a meeting with his two assistants in his office.

'I think it's time for us to take stock of the many incidents in this case,' he said. 'Largely because of Lady Elizabeth's iron control of her own family and the Brantleys having pulled up the drawbridge, all interest in it seems to have evaporated. However, if for any reason, further questions are raised and if we are to learn anything from what has gone on, I have decided that it would be a good idea for us to review what happened.

'Perhaps it would help to get the discussion started if I attempt to disentangle the relationships between those involved. I say attempt advisedly, because they are quite complex.

'First, let me consider Lady Elizabeth. Purely on the grounds of her looks, her height and personality and what James Brantley hinted to me, it seems more than likely that she was not a legitimate member of the Brantley family and quite possibly the result of a fling that her mother had after bearing her husband two sons, the elder being the present Earl and the other his brother, James.

'The previous Earl and his successor being members of Opus Dei meant that Lady Elizabeth was forced to continue her pregnancy that resulted from her rape by the schizophrenic patient, Alan Crosby. He had absconded from the mental hospital some miles away, where he had been a patient for many years and he committed suicide later that night. Before he had been taken ill, his mother had told him that his father was the then Earl, with whom she had had a brief affair during the war. He happened to see the announcement of the ball for Lady Elizabeth's eighteenth birthday in a magazine taken by his mother and that led to him running away from the hospital and attacking and raping her during the night after the event. He hanged himself in a wood nearby later that night.

'Richard Kershaw, a friend of James Brantley, who had been Lady Elizabeth's partner at the ball was persuaded to marry her and to be accepted as the father of the twins. As a quid pro quo, he was set up with her in the house in Highgate with an additional financial settlement, and there was an understanding between him and Lady Elizabeth that they would not have a sexual relationship, but would support each other in other ways. The two children were never told the truth about their real parentage and it also seems likely that the same was the case with their uncle, James Brantley.

'If Alison had been aware of this, would it have enabled her to cope better with Kershaw's abuse and would it even help her now? We have no means of knowing and it has to be Lady Elizabeth's decision and hers alone as to whether it should be brought into the open or not. Either of you have any views? Sarah?'

'What a terrible decision for anyone to have to make! My view is that in most cases, in the long run, the truth is almost always the best option. Would the effects on Alison be eased by knowing that the abuse she suffered was not at the hands of her real father? Would that be balanced by the distress caused by knowing that he was a schizophrenic and the son of James Brantley's father, but at least not one of her own blood relatives. I just don't know, but considering everyone else involved in this sad affair, in particular her own brother and his family, if I were the one to have to make the decision, I would let sleeping dogs lie.'

'Mark?'

'I agree with Sarah. I think it likely that some form of accommodation has already been made by most of those who played a part in the sequence of events and to stir it all up again would, I believe, only add to the misery, rather than relieve it.'

Tyrrell nodded. 'I think you're both right. From what I know or have heard about them, I believe that when Alison Stevens comes out of prison, she will have the support of her mother, her brother and James Brantley. No doubt, too, the admirable Parker will be there for all of them. That leaves the other two players in this sad affair, John Fielding and his wayward wife, Annette.'

Tyrrell looked across the desk at Sarah Prescott and raised his eyebrows a fraction.

'Much as I disliked having to do so,' she said, 'I decided to have a final word with Rebecca Cochrane, who told me what had happened to them. You won't be surprised to hear that they were divorced recently and Fielding made it as easy as possible for his wife. The chosen grounds were irreconcilable differences and, as they had their own bank accounts and very few capital assets, their flat being rented, there was no argument about financial distribution. I asked a lawyer, specializing in divorce, if Annette would have been successful had she gone for maintenance payments, and the answer was that she probably would have been. However, she didn't do so and I imagine that her father, the retired judge, might well have had some input into that decision. I can't see a man in his position being happy about news reports of his daughter having been implicated in adultery with a man, who not only was her husband's senior colleague, but had also been murdered.

'As for Fielding, he has recently obtained a consultant post as a neurosurgeon at a unit in the south of England and good luck to him, I say. I think he behaved with admirable restraint throughout the whole sordid business.'

'Mark, you're the man for the apt quotation. Anything come to mind?'

Sinclair thought for a moment or two. 'There is one in French that stuck in my mind when I was reading modern languages at Oxford. It's from a play by Corneille, entitled *Le Menteur*, the liar. "*Il faut qu'un menteur aît bonne memoir*".'

Tyrrell nodded. 'There's a good deal of truth in that and I have an instinct that if anyone is capable of carrying off this whole affair in the best possible way for all concerned, the redoubtable Lady Elizabeth will be that person.'